Earthdark

MONICA HUG[...]

Returning to the Moon aft[...] [...]t to
Earth, Kepler Masterman f[...] [...] back home
frustratingly sterile. The well-ordered, utilitarian
society on the Moon contrasts grimly with the
freedom and fun he experienced on Earth.

Desperate for adventure Kepler decides to take a
forbidden trip out on to the Moon's surface but
even he did not bargain for the sinister series of
events which he finds himself caught up in.
Narrowly escaping death, he returns to Base only
to find that his girlfriend's father has disappeared.
Fearing for his safety, the two set out for the
strange and unknown region of Earthdark on the
farthest side of the Moon where they believe Ann's
father may be. But something important is taking
place in Earthdark – something which interests
more than one ruthless power – and unaware of the
dangerous forces surrounding them, the young
people walk straight into a trap. . . .

Also by Monica Hughes

Earthdark

MONICA HUGHES

MAMMOTH

First published in Great Britain 1977
By Hamish Hamilton Children's Books Ltd
Magnet paperback edition published 1981
Reissued 1991 by Mammoth
an imprint of Mandarin Paperbacks
Michelin House, 81 Fulham Road, London SW3 6RB

Mandarin is an imprint of the Octopus Publishing Group

ISBN 0 7497 0404 7

A CIP catalogue record for this title
is available from the British Library

Printed and bound in Great Britain by
BPCC Hazell Books
Aylesbury, Bucks, England
Member of BPCC Ltd.

HIGHLIGHTS IN THE
HISTORY OF MOON'S COLONISATION

1959 Luna 2 crashed on Moon
1968 Apollo 8: first manned orbit of Moon
1969 Apollo 11: first landing of men on Moon
1975 Apollo–Soyuz link-up
1980 UN Base set up in Sinus Medii: Russian and U.S. astronauts in cooperation with scientists from G.B., France and Germany
1982 Temporary base set up in Kepler Crater. Work on low-temperature and vacuum engineering started
1983 Development of magnecar. Opening of Imbrium Terminal
1984 Temporary bases in Copernicus and Alphonsus
1985 First permanent base in Kepler Crater
1986 Permanent base established in Copernicus
1989 Permanent base established in Alphonsus
1990 First child born on Moon, son of Governor Masterman
1994 First commercial mining started in Aristarchus
1995 LEMCON obtains UN charter for mineral rights on Moon
1998 Aristarchus declared off-limits to colonists
2000 Start of Genesis Project
2005 Governor Masterman goes to Earth to petition UN
      New UN Mandate
      Completion of Genesis One

To Glen whose dreams go beyond Genesis

Chapter One

IT WAS HIGH NOON when the old Moon ferry touched down at Imbrium Terminal. I had been away for three months, and it felt good to be back on the one-sixth weight Moon where I belonged.

I was happy all the way across to the Sea of Rains Terminal Building. Then our ground transport coupled to a lock entrance and the doors slid open to a narrow tunnel, painted the dull green I remembered so well. Moon green! It was everywhere. But I had forgotten just how dispiriting a colour it was.

The far door opened and we crowded into the concourse dome. It was packed with people waiting to greet my father, the Moon Governor. I recognised Miles Fargo, the big wheel of LEMCON, the Lunar Exploration and Mining Consortium. It was LEMCON, the huge transnational conglomerate, that had shouldered aside the first Moon colonists and taken over the exploitation of Moon's mineral resources. The profits had funnelled into LEMCON's empire back on Earth, and did little for us colonists.

Though you wouldn't know it to see them together, Father and Miles Fargo were enemies: what each wanted for Moon was alien to the other. But the rest of the crowd were friends. Every Moon base was represented. I saw Joe Asaka from Copernicus, and Pierre Laframboise, the manager of the Serenity Hilton. I suppose *he* was worried about what all the talk of Moon independence might do to the tourist trade, which was still our chief source of income.

Sir Michael Stokes, Mick to his friends, had come from the vulcanology station in Alphonsus to talk with Father, and I saw Huntley Sheppard's grey head towering above the others. As Lunar Comptroller he had been in charge while Father and I were down on Earth, and he and Father would have a lot of catching up to do.

What with the Moon representatives and the LEMCON crowd, and the dozen tourists who had come in with us on the Moon ferry and were milling around oohing and aahing at the sights while they waited for their transport to the hotel, it took me a few minutes to realise that Ann Sheppard had not come from Kepler Base with her father to meet me.

In the three months I had been on Earth I'd written to her constantly – well, maybe not that often, so much had been going on – but I'd certainly *thought* about her a lot, especially in the last three weeks on Earth, after Hilary and I had said goodbye. I'd looked forward to telling her about my life under the sea with Uncle Ted, Aunt Janet and Cousin Jon. And Hilary . . .

Perhaps I shouldn't tell Ann much about Hilary. It would be difficult to explain how I'd felt about the girl with red hair and pearl-pale skin without hurting Ann's feelings. Only Ann wasn't even here. She hadn't come to Imbrium Terminal to meet me.

I swallowed and felt my shoulders sag. Father was engulfed in people, all trying to get next to him, all talking at once. He called to me over the crowd as he was swept towards the elevators. "Sorry, Kep. I'll be a while. You'll be all right?"

"Sure, Father. Of course. After all, I'm home now, aren't I?" I grinned until I thought my face would crack. The tourists stared at me respectfully and whispered. Then the bright lights of approaching jets sparked for an instant through the darkened ports. The hotel courier began to herd them towards the airlock at which the luxury jet coach had just coupled. In a few moments they would be coasting along the Apennine Range to the hotel nestled below the eastern ridge of Fresnel Promontory. The lock hatch slid shut and I was alone.

Alone and neglected. I wandered in and out of the observation dome. The sight of Earth, high in the sky near the sun, made me homesick. Homesick? But Moon was home, and I was just being stupid.

I took the elevator down to the deserted cafeteria and punched out an order for soup and sandwich on the auto-chef. The soup was hot and nourishing, a soy-flour base with artificial onion flavour, and the sandwich was filled with a high-protein yeast culture. It was good wholesome food; I'd been eating stuff like it all my life. So why should it suddenly taste like cardboard? And why should my mouth water for Aunt Janet's undersea cooking? I pushed the plate away and brooded...

A sudden noise in the corridor made me look up. The conference room was emptying. Two heads rose above the rest of the crowd, my father's and Huntley Sheppard's. I left my unwanted lunch and elbowed desperately through the crowd.

"Dr Sheppard, where's Ann?" I spoke abruptly, with no thought of moon courtesy.

He blinked at my bad manners, but answered me in his soft Highland voice. "Ann? Why, she's home at Kepler Base, of course. Where would you expect her to be?"

"Here. To meet me. It's been three months, you know."

My voice was too loud and he raised his eyebrows. "Three months Earth-time, Kep. Only three lunar days and nights, remember. But you have changed in that short time, haven't you? Well, cheer up. You'll be seeing Ann soon enough. Today she had work to do."

He turned his back on me and began to talk to Mick Stokes, leaving me alone in the middle of the crowd, with my overlong Earth-style hair and my ears flaming with embarrassment.

Luckily I wasn't stuck there for long. The transport for

Kepler Base arrived. Father extracted himself from what looked like a heavy encounter with the LEMCON men, and we took the elevator up to the concourse and locked through to our magnecar. To my surprise the Comptroller stayed behind, so that Father and I were alone.

I thought he would rip into me for my bad manners, but all he said was, "You'll have to get used to Moon ways again, Kep. Take it easy until you've found your feet. I've enjoyed the free and easy Earth manners too, but we have to remember that on Moon we have a closed and controlled society. There just isn't enough room to rub people the wrong way."

I hadn't seen too much of him since Mother died and he became Governor, but he was still a terrific father and the kindest man I knew. I left him working his way through a brief-case crammed with papers and walked forward to the driver's compartment. I took the seat beside Tim O'Connor and watched the moonscape unfold ahead of us on the television monitors.

"How have things been up here for the last three months, Tim?"

"So-so." He shrugged, his eyes on the monitors. "Your father's done great work for us down at the UN, but, mark my words, LEMCON will turn nasty."

"Turn nasty?" I repeated. "What on Moon can they do? Now the UN has given us the mandate to run our own affairs, including the mines, what can LEMCON do except go along with it?"

"I don't know." Tim shrugged again. "But a driver gets to hear things as he moves around. And the word is that the miners in Aristarchus are talking pretty wildly. They've got a stake in Moon too, you know. It's an awfully long way to come for eighteen months' work, away from Earth and their families."

"They get paid plenty, I hear."

"They earn it, Kep. It's a tough life, lonely and dangerous. If Moon colony gets its fair share of the mining profits, you can bet it won't come out of the pockets of LEMCON shareholders back on Earth. They'll scrape it out of the miners' bonuses, or pare down safety conditions. There's been talk of LEMCON laying off men, or even pulling right out of lunar exploration and going back to Earth."

I shook my head. "That's crazy. They need our minerals desperately. After all, the big powers on Earth have about scraped the bottom of the barrel there. What little is left belongs to the developing nations, and they need every scrap for themselves if they're to get ahead."

"I hope that never comes to the test, Kep. When the small guy's got the doughnut and the big fellow's hungry, you don't need a crystal ball to guess what'll happen."

Tim checked our position and changed course to the south-west. We were no longer running across the relative flatness of the Mare Imbrium, but between craters, some only big enough to lose a wheel, some almost as large as Kepler Crater. I knew the road would be rough for the next fifty miles. I left him to it and went back to see how Father was doing. When I told him Tim's ideas about LEMCON's reaction his smile seemed a little forced.

"Tim sounds like an echo of Miles Fargo."

"LEMCON's manager? Was he furious at the UN's decision?"

"You'd hardly expect him to be delighted. But he's a realist. He knew this would come sooner or later. Moon colony is almost a quarter of a century old, and for the last ten years LEMCON has been sucking it dry. They've climbed on the backs of our hard-won lunar technology. They've used up our natural resources and made enormous profits, all without paying a cent in royalties. Of course it couldn't last, and Miles Fargo knows it."

"But you're afraid that won't stop him fighting anyway?" I stared at him. "Father, what would you do if the miners got out of hand?"

He stared at me in turn, his shaggy eyebrows raised. "If anything like that were to happen, I would expect the mining police to control it," he said quietly.

"But suppose they didn't? Suppose LEMCON just let the men

rip? Father, we don't even have our own police force!"

"Thank God we've never needed one. Twenty-five years without a crime is a wonderful record. I hope we can maintain it – I believe we can. If everyone keeps their head. *Everyone*, Kep." He opened another file and settled his glasses on his nose, leaving me to worry about the mandate, about LEMCON, and about Ann.

But when we arrived at Kepler Crater, the Moon base where I had been born, the first child born on Moon, Ann was waiting for me. There must have been fifty people there, but she was the only one I saw. She felt very small and fragile in my arms, and I realised how much muscle I had acquired in my life under the sea. "I'm sorry, Ann. I didn't mean to squeeze you to death."

She drew back, her pale face flushed. "Kep, everyone's looking."

"Bother everyone. Oh, Ann, I've missed you so much."

"Yes. Well, of course so have I," she murmured. "But really, Kep. Showing emotion in public? Where are your moon manners?"

It was my turn to blush. My arms fell awkwardly to my sides. "I'm sorry. It was just . . ."

She smiled primly and smoothed her already neat hair. Her eyes were large and dark and beautiful . . . only it was a pity that they didn't light up when she smiled. Like Hilary's.

I pushed the thought from my mind. "Why didn't you meet me at Imbrium? I really missed you."

"With people staring? All the talk about your exploits on Earth? Oh, I couldn't. But I'm free now. I've my lunch break, and maybe this once I could miss my study period." She smiled at me kindly, and walked towards the elevators, straight, self-contained, elegant even in the buff tunic and pants that were lunar uniform.

I was really very lucky, I told myself firmly as I followed her into the elevator. "It's great to be home," I said aloud.

Chapter Two

GREAT TO BE HOME! During the next seven watches of the lunar day and the fourteen watches of the following night I kept telling myself just how good it was to be back home on Moon. Every time I said it, to myself or aloud to my old moon friends, I sounded grimmer and grimmer.

I was mad at myself too. Moon had always seemed to me the best place in the whole solar system in which to grow up. Now all of a sudden everything seemed to have gone sour. I found myself getting edgy as I stood in line in cafeteria or waiting for the washroom facilities, and I swore in a very unlunar fashion when the metered amount of shower water was used up before I was through, leaving me standing in the shower stall covered with soap suds.

My six-foot-square sleep cubicle was like a prison, and I began to feel that if I ever saw another green-painted wall or ceiling I would go into space frenzy. There must have been enough green paint on Kepler Base to colour the whole Ocean of Storms.

I kept thinking about the cosy living room down on Conshelf Ten, with its crimson drapes and cushions and the wonderful flame-coloured rug that Aunt Janet had hooked. I even talked about it to Ann. I felt that maybe *she* would understand.

She stared at me as if I were out of my mind. "Hook a rug? Why in the world would anyone want to spend valuable time doing that? What would be the use of it? The floor is always comfortably warm down here."

"Does everything have to be useful? Once in a while couldn't we just do things because they're fun? Because it feels good."

She thought about it carefully, her face grave. Then, "Kep,

13

dear." She didn't usually speak to me so gently. "Kep, have you thought about talking to one of the staff psychologists? Ever since you got back from Earth . . ." She shrugged and let the sentence hang there.

"Why do you think there's something wrong with *me*, just because I can see that Kepler Base is dreary and ugly and no fun to live in? All of you, you're so complacent it's unreal. Ann, think. *You* can remember Earth. It's only five years since your family came up to Moon. Remember what it was like back there, and then look at this."

We were standing in the cafeteria at the time. 'A' watch had just finished dinner and the room was almost empty. We both had lectures to attend and should be on our way, but I held her back.

"Just look at it." I waved my arm.

The forty tables stood in two neat rows on the green vinyl floor. Their white surfaces gleamed. No flowers, no tablecloths, not so much as a bottle of ketchup marred the symmetry. Over to the right the stainless steel food servers were being scrubbed and polished in readiness for the men and women of 'C' watch who would be coming in for breakfast in an hour.

"Look at it, Ann. It's got no soul."

"It's perfectly efficient, Kep. What else would you want?"

"It's so tasteless. It's like the food. Ann, I'm sure life up here could be better if we'd only try and use some imagination."

"Better? You don't have any idea of how good life is up here. Honestly, Kep, you've come back to Moon talking like some big Earth expert. But what did you actually *see* in three months? You saw the inside of one luxury hotel and an undersea colony. Well, you listen to me, Kepler Masterman. I was only nine when we came to Moon, but I can remember what Earth was *really* like. The overcrowding. The smell of poverty. Everybody clawing at each other for a little more of what was left of the good life. No thank you, Kep. I'm thankful we're on Moon, and if it has to be this way, then that's the way I like it."

She stalked out of the cafeteria then and I didn't bring up the subject again. But I was late for my next class — again.

Two days later, though, as we were going up to the twelfth

floor Astronomy Section, she said quite casually, "By the way, Kep, I'm arranging to transfer over to 'B' watch for the next few months."

It didn't dawn on me for a minute. "Yes?" I said, and then did a double take. It was unusual even for adults to change from their originally assigned watch, and kids and students never did. We were automatically on the same watch as our parents, and grew up together, with the same friends, eating meals together, studying and working together, and sharing the same recreational facilities. Even our sleep cubicles were all on the same floor.

Dormitory A was on the third floor, nearly at the bottom of Kepler Base, with only the maintenance engineering facilities, the cosmic storm shelter and the water and oxygen storage tanks below. Dormitory B was on the fourth floor and Dormitory C above it on the fifth. For eight out of every twenty-four hours one of the three sleep floors would be in darkness, while one third of the total personnel of Kepler Base slept.

It was an efficient system, but it had some odd social effects. Of the twelve hundred people on Kepler Base most of us knew only the four hundred on our own watch. The others you might meet occasionally in the corridors or the recreation areas, or at special times like the New Day parties, or when some important visiting lecturer from Earth came up. I can only remember one occasion of a marriage between two scientists on different moon watches, and they had known each other on Earth before coming to Moon. In all my fifteen years on Kepler Base I'd never even got off the elevator at the fourth or fifth floor.

So now I just stared at Ann. "You can't transfer!"

"Of course I can, Kep. It's all been arranged."

"That must have taken some doing. Did you get your father to pull strings?"

"That's not fair, Kep. I never bring your father up at you."

"I'm sorry. I didn't mean it. But, Ann, why. . .?"

"I went to some lectures by Guy Roget while you were down on Earth. Didn't I tell you?" Ann's usually pale cheeks were suddenly faintly pink, and I had the feeling that she wasn't being completely honest with me. "He's offering a special course in celestial mechanics which I really want to get. I can't fit it into my 'A watch schedule, but with a bit of juggling I can do it on 'B' ".

"And it's *that* important? Just a crummy course?"

"He's really very good."

I stared at her blankly. Guy Roget? I *knew* she'd never mentioned him before. He was just an excuse, a polite reason for changing watch. It had to be me. For some reason Ann wanted to get away from me. Only . . .

"Ann!"

"No, don't, Kep."

My eyes dropped. "You're really transferring? When?"

"Tomorrow, actually. I'll work my watch in the morning and move my stuff over to 'B' when their wake-up light goes on at 1500."

"Do you need any help?"

"No thanks, Kep. I haven't got much."

None of us did, of course. A change or two of uniform, some toiletries, a few microbooks, a personal photograph or two. It would all fit into one small suitcase – the accumulation of fourteen years. But that's how it was on Moon, everything pared down to the bare essentials.

"I won't be able to see you at all. I wish you'd told me what you were planning. I'd have arranged to go too. Maybe it's not too late. Maybe I could ask for a transfer too."

"No, don't do that, Kep. It wouldn't be a good idea."

"I don't see why not."

"Well, for one thing your father'd be alone."

"Father? That's funny. I see less of him now than I will of you. If it comes to that, what about *your* family? Won't they miss you?"

"That's different. Mother and Daddy have each other. Anyway, you've got an awful lot of catching up to do in your computer courses. If you switched watches you'd only get further behind."

"I suppose so. But I will miss you, Ann."

She smiled her small neat smile and looked up at me with those dark space-empty eyes. "Work hard, Kep. Maybe without any distractions you'll do better. And I'm only transferring for three months. Then . . ."

'Then?"

"Then we'll see. I must go, Kep. I'm going to be late for class."

She hurried down the corridor to Astrophysics, leaving me standing by the elevators with my mouth open. When I looked down I realised that I'd left my books somewhere again, and I couldn't remember where. I couldn't remember which class I was supposed to be in either.

In a way it was a relief not having to live up to Ann, but I badly needed a friend to talk to, and now that Ann was gone there didn't seem to be anybody else. We had always been a tightly knit group, the forty of us that made up the teen-age population of 'A' watch. But it seemed that in the three months that I had been away on Earth they had flowed together into the space that I had left, and now there was no longer any room for me, not with the same sort of closeness that there had been before.

The others seemed to have changed, too. It wasn't only Ann who was different. Life on Kepler was so serious and sparse. Lectures, lab work, long discussions on the socio-economic future of Moon. Even their hobbies seemed to be just off-shoots of school work, things like plant genetics or astronomy. Some of them did play chess, but I just didn't have the patience.

I looked round the rec room next free period and realised that not one of my friends was resting or being lazy, or doing something just for the fun of it. I watched them for a long time. It was as if I'd never seen them before. It was the strangest feeling, as if I were a visitor from another planet. Had I ever been that deadly serious about everything, I wondered?

After a while I went up to stores and drew out some paper and glue and balsa wood. I sat down at one of the small tables in rec and began to build myself a tower. I couldn't get it started right. I was nervous and my mind kept getting in the way. But after a while my fingers took over and the tower began to grow right. It became tall and slender and fantastical. When it was finished I decorated it with crystal-shaped cut-outs of coloured tissue.

It was thirty inches high. It swayed elegantly under moon-grav and the tissue crystals shimmered. The others began to drop what they were doing and come over to my table. Soon there was a crowd.

"What is it?"

"A tower, of course."

"Well, we can see that. But what's it *for*?"

"Would you believe – for fun?"

"Oh, come on, Kep!"

Jerry looked at it with his head critically tilted. "It would make a good mooring mast for dirigibles," he suggested.

"If only we had an atmosphere," someone else put in.

"Or what about a diving tower?"

"If the seas only held water!"

They laughed. For a second or two the fragile gaiety of my tower touched them. But as they began to realise that it really *was* perfectly useless and didn't have some subtle purpose that I was keeping from them, they drifted back to their own occupations. Only Wanda put out a finger and touched it gently, almost regretfully.

Paul stopped beside me long enough to remind me kindly that I was wasting valuable colony material on a project that could give no useful return.

"It won't be wasted," I snapped at him.

"Well, tell us what it's *for* then."

I felt like telling him that it was really a hooked rug, but I knew he'd never begin to understand and sooner or later I'd wind up in the head shrink's office, so I held my peace and let him have the last word.

I carried the tower carefully down to my sleep cubicle and put it on the small chest that besides the bed was the only furniture the room contained. It looked very frail and gay against the dull green walls and the painted metal furniture and the grey thermo-blanket. It nodded and shimmered in the faint air from the ventilation duct. Quite suddenly the room became mine. Mine and nobody else's. I felt as if I'd just made an enormous discovery.

I went straight up to Father's office in the seventh floor Admin wing. I just had to talk to him and find out what was going on inside my head. If I didn't talk I felt I would burst or run up the walls or *something*.

18

He wasn't there.

I just stood. His secretary, Thomasina McLeod, Tommy for short, must have thought I hadn't heard her.

"He's not on the Base at all, Kep," she repeated.

"When did he leave?"

"A couple of days ago. You didn't know?"

I tried to grin. "Nobody ever tells me anything, Tommy. I don't think I've seen Father for more than a couple of minutes at a time since we got back."

"He *has* been frantically busy with the Mandate, Kep."

"I know. It's not his fault. Where did he go? Maybe I could hop the next levicar and see him. Or phone him even . . ." My voice trailed off at her expression.

"But he's in Aristarchus, Kep."

"LEMCON's complex?" I was startled. Even before the recent tension the colonists and scientists of the moon bases kept themselves strictly away from the mining operations. And vice versa. I wondered what on Moon Father could be doing in Aristarchus.

"Yes." There was a silence in which Tommy fiddled with the things on her desk. Then she looked up at me. "Look, Kep, I don't think it's such a great idea phoning your father. Not just now. You'd be almost sure to catch him in conference. Can't it wait?"

"I suppose it'll have to. I guess I should have made an appointment." I laughed sarcastically.

"That's not a bad idea, Kep." Tommy's face was perfectly serious. "Look, I'm really not sure when he'll be back, but I'll make a note of it and fit you in *somewhere*. Would half an hour be enough time?"

"An hour, if it's not too much to ask."

Again the sarcasm seemed to escape her. "I'll see what I can do." She smiled and went back to her work.

There was nothing else for me to do but walk nonchalantly out past all the desks of the typing pool, tripping over my own feet in the doorway.

Maybe I should write him a note, I thought, and leave it in his sleep cubicle.

Dear Father,
When you have a moment to spare between the heavy chores of running Moon, conciliating LEMCON and chivvying the UN, I would be grateful for a short interview. I am coming apart at the seams.

   Your distracted son, Kepler
P.S. Remember me?

Oh, forget it. Maybe if I concentrated on my work I'd forget all my problems too. That's what the shrinks would say, I knew. I should get on with studying those infernal computer circuits.

I didn't, though. Instead, I took the elevator all the way up to the dome. It was deserted and I slipped up the stairs into the observation bubble almost guiltily. Another time waste.

The rough surface of Kepler Crater was bathed in the silver magic of earthshine. It was almost midnight, and Earth was nearly full. I glanced at the wall thermometer. The temperature outside was minus a hundred and twenty degrees Celsius and dropping. By dawn, seven watch days away, it would have dropped another fifty degrees

The stars burned fiercely, crowding the distant sky, while high in the east, so close that I felt it might fall at any minute, Earth, an inch-wide silver disc, hung above my head. I stared up at it. It stared right back at me, a great eye in the sky, unmoving, always hovering overhead, like my conscience monitoring even my thoughts.

I pushed the idea out of my mind. It wasn't really like that at all. Earth wasn't an enemy. My friends were there.

A brilliant patch of light on its surface caught my attention. I couldn't recognise the continents for sure in this phase, but it looked to me as if that bright patch was the clouds of a storm centre developing in the Bay of Mexico. If so, up there, just a bit to the north and east, must be Conshelf Ten.

It would be mid-morning there now and they would be busy in the labs, or out in the kelp beds or the fish farms. How I missed them all. Uncle Ted, Aunt Janet. Jon. In spite of the nightmare things that had happened to me, in spite of my trial and capture, we had managed to have so much fun. There always seemed to have been time, down there under the sea. Time to stop and look. Time to sit and talk.

And then there was Hilary. But maybe it would be better not even to think about Hilary.

Earth glared down at me with its bright watchful eye. I got up guiltily. Time to go below and do some hard studying before to-morrow's classes.

Chapter Three

I DIDN'T SEE ANN, even for a minute, until the new day dawned a week later. The Moon kids held a party every New Day. It had been a tradition from the beginning, as it was a tradition that some-one newly come up from Earth would tease us. "You kids are spoiled. Imagine a party every day!"

But of course it wasn't every day, not every *watch* day. It was only twelve or thirteen times a year, and not really an extrava-gance. We'd save some of our biscuit ration through the week before, so nothing was wasted, and the little ones just loved it. The party was always held in the cafeteria, the only room on Kepler Base big enough to hold the kids of all three watches, and the only room, except for Surface Security, to have view ports on all four sides.

I didn't see Ann at first. I was with the other "A" watch kids as we watched the shimmering stream of pearly light pour from the corona in the seconds before the dawn. The old magic was still there. The sun's first rays turned the crater rim to a line of white flame. The shadows ran black as night across the crater floor to the dome itself. Then, with a glare like an old style atom bomb, the sun itself exploded into sight. Night was over. Everyone cheered. Someone put on a music tape and the dancing began.

I didn't want to dance, not right away. I sat at a table by myself to savour the New Day feeling. I could feel it in the air, in the table, in the floor. I could feel the changes, as Kepler Base adjusted from the long two weeks of night to the two weeks of day to come. I could feel it as if I were a part of the building myself.

I was on the surface where the bank of solar cells absorbed the sun's energy, storing it in batteries and hot water tanks, our insurance against the night to come. I was in Hydroponics, as the new sun bathed the eight miles of plastic tubing that contained the Base's algae supply, algae for food, oxygen and air purification. I was in Astronomy as the men on Sun Watch manned their consoles, searching for solar storms, for now as day dawned, unprotected by atmosphere, we were in constant danger of fall-out from the biggest nuclear furnace of them all — the sun itself.

The music played and the kids danced. Beneath my hands I could feel the whole of Kepler Base as if it were an extension of my own finger tips. I was part of it. It was part of me.

A couple of four-year olds crashed into the table. Some of the small ones were getting pretty wild. At moon-grav dancing could get out of hand pretty easily. It didn't take much energy to whirl around off your feet, but the pain of slamming into a wall or a metal table wasn't diminished a bit. I scooped them up and handed them over to one of the kindergarten supervisors, who soothed their yells with extra biscuits.

Then I saw Ann. She was dancing with a guy I didn't recognise. One of her new friends on 'B' watch, I supposed. I cut in on them without ceremony.

"Happy New Day, Ann!"

"Happy Day, Kep."

We danced in silence for a while, hardly moving to the music, almost floating. She was looking at her most calm and beautiful. I wanted to tell her my feelings about the Base and the new day. Would she be able to share my sense of one-ness with the organism that we called home? Not down here for sure, not in all this crowd and noise.

"Come with me, Ann." I pulled her hand and she followed me off the dance floor.

"Where to?"

"Up to the dome. I want to go to the dome."

"Why, Kep? Why go up six floors when you can see it all on the view screens right here?"

"It's not the same, Ann. One's real, the other's . . . canned. And I want to talk to you alone, Ann."

23

"All right, then." She shrugged. "You haven't changed a bit, have you, Kep?" Her tone of voice made it clear that it wasn't a compliment.

From up in the observation bubble we could look right down on the crater floor and at the terminator that bisected it. To the east everything was bathed in white light except for the deep shadow cast by the crater rim on that side. To the west was night, except for the rim of fire at the top of the crater. Long shadows ran across like dark fingers, as if the night was trying to cling on and not let itself be pushed away, while high spots of moon rock over in night caught the sun and cheated the dawn coming. It was a crazy kaleidoscope of black and white.

Suddenly I felt I needed to be right out there, to be part of Moon. "Look, Ann." I pointed down. "There's a two-man crawler parked at lock four. Let's sneak out and go for a ride." I grabbed her hands and begged her with my eyes.

"For no reason? Without permission?" She pulled her hands away. "Kep, you *are* crazy."

"Maybe I am. Maybe we're all crazy up here. Back on Earth Hil . . . some of the people used to call me lunatic because I was from Moon. It was just a joke, but maybe. . . Ann, I want to go out and ride the terminator. I haven't done it in years. Have you? When did you last go out for a dawn ride?"

She shook her head. "I don't know. Ages. I've forgotten."

"How could you *forget*. Come on, Ann. Come with me."

"You know we're not allowed to go joy-riding without parental permission."

"Father's away. By the time I get to see him it'll probably be the middle of the night again. All right, then. You ask your father. Ask him for both of us, and we'll go."

She shook her head. "No, I won't. I don't want to. There's no point in it."

The frustration in me boiled up and spilled over. "Okay, then, I'll go by myself. Please, Ann. Come with me. I'm going whether you come or not, but please . . ."

Her face closed like a door slamming. "You *are* mad. I certainly will not come. I'm going back down to the party right now.

24

You'd better forget all this nonsense and come too. If you go outside I'll have to report you. You know that."

I stared at her. Her eyes dropped. I shrugged and turned away. "I guess that's up to you, Ann. But look, at least give me a little time out there before you turn me in, all right?"

She came up to me then. Her eyes were sparkling in the east light.

"Ann, you're not *crying*, are you?" It was as disconcerting as if moon rock had begun to melt.

"Of course I'm not, silly. I never cry. The light's too strong, that's all. That window's not dimming properly. All right, Kep. I'll give you half an hour. Then I'm going to have to go to Security. Please be back before then, and maybe they won't be too angry with you."

She turned and ran down the steps and across the concourse to the elevators. As the door slid shut behind her I closed the observation bubble hatch and went into the change room for my spacesuit. First the close-fitting elastic mesh thermal anti-vacuum suit and then on top of it the loose light-weight aluminised outer suit with its double-soled boots, gas-tight gauntlets and helmet. I checked the heat exchange, the oxygen supply and the carbon dioxide "scrubber" and then I went out and punched the release button connecting lock four to the crawler car.

These two-man crawlers were different again from the magnecars and levicars, and from the cargo jets and luxury carriers. They were made of a very strong light-weight alloy, with a plastic dome cover and a one-man air-lock.

Their short range visibility was very good, but there were no sleeping, cooking or toilet facilities. They ran on battery power and a small jet engine with a theoretical five-hundred-mile fuel range, but they were intended strictly as taxis, for shuttling scientists from the base to surface facilities, or for local data collecting.

I strapped myself into the driver's seat, checked the atmosphere and the integrity of the seals and then detached myself from the airlock. Now it was safe to push back my visor and take off my clumsy gauntlets. Running on batteries alone I moved slowly into the safety zone and then ignited the burners.

The crawler trembled under me and moved slowly forward across the crater floor. There wasn't a soul around. I was in luck.

As I neared the debris-strewn walls of Kepler Crater I tipped the jets and responsively the car lifted, half hovering, half crawling on its tracks, up the fifty-five degree slope. It was the trickiest part of the trip, next to getting back down again into Kepler on my return. It took both hands, both feet and a lot of practice to keep a crawler level, balancing the lift against the forward thrust so that I neither flipped over backwards or nosed into solid rock.

I'd had a lot of practice in all my years on Moon, but never alone, and my hands were sweating by the time I'd made it to the top. I switched off, and settled slowly on the ridge of the rim, the wide treads of the crawler holding securely to the dusty rock.

I wiped off my face and hands and looked north along the curve of the terminator. From up here, on the rim of Kepler, two thousand feet above the basalt surface of the Ocean of Storms, I could see thirty miles, unimpeded by smoke, fog, dust or even air itself, clear to the curve of the horizon and the black universe beyond.

Over to my left, towards night, the surface was a jumble of black and white, impossible to make sense of, where a lump of breccia the size of my fist might catch the sun in a blinding dazzle or cast a shadow so long and dense that it looked like a crevasse slashing the surface of the *mare*. Over to my right all detail was lost in a white glare, painful even through the darkened plastic bubble.

Right ahead of me, in places where the sun shone angled and shadowless on the smooth *mare*, I could just see the faint rays of ash, feather pale against the dark basalt, which streaked out from Kepler Crater.

Due north of me ran one streak as wide and straight as a super highway. Two hundred miles away, over the horizon, it touched and was touched, I knew, by one of the rays of ash thrown out over ten thousand years ago from Aristarchus.

The gossamer line of ash beckoned me. Be back in half an hour, Ann had begged, but I hadn't promised anything. Due north around the curve of Moon the terminator stretched. I knew I shouldn't go. If I were to turn back now I might even slip down

26

and join the party and nobody would be the wiser. But the invisible road beckoned.

A hundred miles north and a hundred miles back, I promised myself. Not a mile more. Just a couple of hours to be alone and get my head together. And anyway, if I *did* get into serious trouble with Security and I was almost bound to, well then maybe Father would find the time to come and talk to me.

The sun shone white and hot against the side of the crawler, and the coolers whined into operation. At this height I couldn't see what I'd come out to see anyway. I started the crawler up again and tipped carefully down the gentle outer slope of the crater to the surface of the *mare*. Still nothing to see. I headed due north.

I'd been out for almost an hour before it happened, the moon-dawn phenomenon we kids used to call "star-dust". One moment it wasn't there. The next, right ahead of me, to left and right, the whole surface of the *mare* shattered into a million points of shimmering light, scintillating in white and blue, green and red. I stopped the crawler and sat in the silence of moon surface to watch.

It was like the library micro-film I'd once seen of fire-works, only there was no noise and no smoke. And it went on. And on. There was no sound but the quiet shushing of the cooling system and the occasional minute *ping* as a particle of stellar dust vaporised against the meteor barrier of the crawler. The lights winked on and off, shimmered, vanished, reappeared.

I used to tell the small fry, when they first came out to see the dawn spectacle, that when the angels swept the stars clean at the start of each new day the star-dust fell on Moon and sparkled there. It was what my mother had told me, the first child born on Moon, in the years we were together, before she died.

It had always been my dream, as it was the dream of every little moon child, to capture a speck or two of star-dust and keep them safe in a jar, for ever twinkling. When I grew older I realised that star-dust was like happiness. You couldn't bottle it.

Later still I learned the scientific fact that the various minerals scattered in the surface dust of Moon, bombarded by protons drifting on the solar wind, were excited into fluorescence by the ultra-violet radiation of the rising sun. How dull the facts were. How beautiful the display. I wished it could go on for ever, but I knew it wouldn't last. It was like Earth-dew on a cobweb, but its beauty was unforgettable.

In all my sixteen years on Moon I'd never seen a display to match this one. It was as if Moon were putting on a special celebration to welcome me home, the celebration no one else had given me. I sat in a happy daze as the terminator moved imperceptibly leftwards. I might have sat there until I ran out of air and the terminator vanished over the horizon if I hadn't been jarred out of my dream by the alarm buzzer.

It cut through my thoughts as sharp as a knife slash, as harsh as sandpaper across the skin. I jumped and automatically reached out to flick the radio on to "receive", where it should have been all this time, only I'd needed the peace and quiet.

On Moon each moment of our lives was lived close to that greater reality of death. We worked on the surface under temperatures that varied from minus one hundred and seventy degrees Celsius at predawn to a blistering hundred and thirty above at noon. We existed in an atmosphere one tenth of a billionth of that of Earth's, a vacuum more perfect than any laboratory on Earth could manufacture. The surface of Moon was a waterless wasteland swept by solar winds. They were not like the winds of Earth, breezes, gales or even hurricanes. They were invisible unfeelable streams of deadly solar particles thrown out by the Sun at unbelievable speeds. And, unlike Earth, Moon had no layer of ozone, no atmosphere of any kind, to hold them back.

So the alarm buzzer was part of our life. It could *be* our life. Its particular warbling note could cut through work, conversation, sleep. It cut through my dreams now, and as one hand went out to the toggle switch on the radio the other snapped shut the visor of my space helmet.

"Attention, all surface personnel. Return to base at once and take cover. Solar storm imminent. ETA Kepler Crater fifty minutes. Five zero minutes. Return to base all surface personnel."

The message was repeated twice. Towards the end the radio hissed and the words were garbled. The advance parties of the solar storm, faster moving than the deadly protons, were already interfering with reception. X-radiation could be stopped by the metal skin of the crawler, but nothing less than forty feet of solid rock would protect me from the shower of protons that would follow. If I didn't want a lethal dose I would have to find shelter fast.

In the first split second of panic my hands went to the controls, ready to gun the jets and turn and run for home. Then reason took over. I took a deep shaky breath and spent a precious thirty seconds checking the clock and the inertial navigator. I'd gone almost a hundred miles north and a point or two west. In that time the line of the terminator had also been moving westward at a steady ten miles an hour. To get back to Kepler would take me an hour, and I'd be heading into full sunlight, right into the path of the storm.

I spent another minute checking the map. North-west, nearly three times as far from me as Kepler Base, was the mining complex of Aristarchus. Three times as far, but Aristarchus was still in night. If I headed for Aristarchus I'd be heading away from the storm instead of into it. If all went well I could get there and seek shelter in the LEMCON compound before the proton storm struck.

It took me another two minutes to lay in a course and double check it. I reset the inertial navigator. Then I gunned the jets and set out for Aristarchus just as fast as the crawler would take me.

Chapter Four

WITH A KIND of careful desperation I drove that crawler across the *mare* towards Aristarchus. It was two hundred miles of basalt, coated with talc-fine moon-dust, which tended to mask over the multitude of small cracks and rilles, any one of which could spell disaster for me if I hit it too hard or at the wrong angle.

The dawn light was my saving. As the sun rose slowly over to my right, almost thirty times as slowly as back on Earth, the long shadows outlined every lava tube, every boulder, every crater from those the size of a soap bubble to those bigger than football stadiums. High in the sky, in its accustomed position, Earth back-lit the shadows and reduced the intensity to a mid-brown.

But it was a terrifying drive. I kept one eye glued to the speedometer and the other to the trackless waste ahead of me, trying to hold a speed that would still give me time to react to the unexpected.

Always in my mind was the knowledge of the approaching storm. There was nothing to see. It wasn't like a hurricane lashing white water up the Atlantic seaboard. It wasn't like a sandstorm dropping choking death out of the Sahara. It was invisible, inaudible. If it overtook me I wouldn't know it. I wouldn't feel a thing. If I were still out on the surface when the cosmic storm jetted past, the protons, caught in Moon's gravitational field like billions of invisible mini-moons, would tear through my body without slowing down enough to measure.

And I still wouldn't know. Only the tell-tale strip of film above the breast pocket of my uniform would darken. Within a few hours I would start to feel dizzy, nauseated, weak. If I were within reach of a hospital lab a massive and irreversible loss of white blood cells would show up. Not that it would matter, since they wouldn't be able to do anything about it.

I bucked across the *mare* in the crawler with death breathing over my shoulder. I was almost back into night now. Only an occasional flare of sunlight reflected to me from a higher than usual crater rim. I drove on into the dark.

Aristarchus should be right ahead of me now, if I hadn't miscalculated. I shifted cautiously and eased the grip of my hands on the controls. The seat was incredibly hard and my legs were beginning to cramp. Crawlers had never been designed for long trips like this, and they had none of the built-in comforts of the brollies or the jet cruisers. To my pressing need to escape the storm had been added what seemed to be at least as important a need – to get to a washroom.

I had been out on the surface now for three hours and was well into dark night. In that time the terminator had crept some thirty miles west of Kepler Base. Was I home free? I had to remind myself that the solar particles, hurtling into space at enormous speeds from some solar explosion, would travel in straight lines unless acted upon by some other force. Moon's gravitational field was such a force. The solar particles could whip around Moon's surface in advance of the visible disc of the sun.

Ahead of me the surface of the *mare* changed. It began to rise almost imperceptibly. There were more loose boulders and rocks. I had to slow down to a crawl to thread my way safely between them. In the darkness my eyes caught a faint shining, like underwater phosphorescence. I had done it! I was seeing the dust of Aristarchus, rich in fluorescent willemite.

I crawled up the crater rim, blinked and slowed to a stop. Were my eyes playing tricks on me? I had been in Aristarchus years before when I was just a kid, before LEMCON had come to Moon, and I could still remember how it had looked, the twenty-nine mile diameter crater, centred with a peak, whose pre-dawn glow, Father had told me, was visible on Earth.

The peak was still there, but eroded by excavators, and its glow would never be noticed. The whole crater floor seemed to be

31

swarming with lights. It was as if I had swum into a cave full of luminous fish, which scattered in all directions at my approach. There was no sound, of course. There was no atmosphere to carry sound, but as I sat watching the scurry of vehicles I could feel the tremor of the heavy machinery below me.

So this was LEMCON. This was the lunar headquarters of the consortium which was tearing all the valuable minerals out of our Moon, paying us no royalties and even charging us Earth-rates for the oxides we needed for oxygen extraction and taxing us for every ounce of water we consumed, water that was in fact a by-product of their refineries.

LEMCON's operations were off-limits to us colonists, and I felt like an intruder, perched in my crawler on the crater rim. Even while I watched, the vehicles all headed in one direction, to a point directly below me. My heart jumped. What had I done? Were they coming to get me? But then I realised that they were probably responding to the same solar warning I had heard earlier, and were going below ground for shelter.

Another fear struck me. If they were all below ground by the time I got down to the crater I might not be able to find an air-lock entrance, or having found it, not be able to operate it.

I started my jets and tipped my crawler carefully down over the rocky rim. There was a well-used road on the far side, firmly compacted of pulverised moon rock, beaten down by the treads of heavy vehicles. It hairpinned to and fro towards the crater floor, so much deeper than Kepler. At one moment my left hand was to the crater wall and my right side hung out over the lights below. The next moment the positions were reversed. Right. Then left. Right again. I zigzagged down. The cab was getting stuffy or something. I kept yawning and my head was starting to spin.

I eased the car on to the more or less level crater floor and looked around me. Most of the machines stood abandoned, their clawlike shovels swinging loosely like dead lobsters. Where were the entrances to the complex?

A monstrous dinosaur of an excavator whirred up to me, its lights flashing. The lights doubled, quadrupled, spun around in a dizzying circle and then suddenly went out.

When I came to I was being dragged through an air-lock hatch. My helmet was off and there was a mask over my face. I put my hand to it, pushing it against my mouth and nose, sucking greedily at the pure oxygen. The lights steadied to a gentle rocking, like a boat in a low swell. I shut my eyes and let whoever it was strip off my space-suit and pull me to my feet.

"I wanna washroom," I managed to croak. Then I was given some water, genuine fresh water, not re-cycled, and then I fell face down on to the wonderful softness of a bed. It tilted under me and shot me off into sleep.

I don't know how long I slept, but I came to myself all of a piece, knowing where I was and why. I opened my eyes cautiously and peered through the lids, straight into the cold grey eyes of the man who was staring at me.

It was all I could do not to jump, but some instinct kept me quiet. He wasn't so close after all. He was standing on the other side of a glass door, no more than five feet from me. A shadow blocked the door and then moved back. Another man.

They were big, both of them, close to the cut-off weight limit for space flight, I'd guess. The one with the grey eyes seemed to have more fat than muscle. His plump face was pink and his hair so fair as to be almost white. With the addition of a fluffy beard he'd have made a pretty good Santa Claus, until you saw those eyes. They were flat grey, as cold and lifeless as moon pebbles.

The second man turned and I saw his face, tanned and seamed with years of sun. His nose jutted from his face and his eyes were blue above the high cheek-bones. His short hair was a carroty red.

I couldn't hear a word. The door was a good fit. But it was obvious from their faces and the movements of their hands that they were arguing. Through my half-closed eyes I began to watch . . .

Us moon kids had picked up some unusual skills, things we took for granted, but that might surprise outsiders. Lip reading was one of them. When you're on the surface in a moon-suit and have something private to say, something you don't want to broadcast over the whole station intercom system, well, almost in self-defence you learn to lip read. So, though they never knew it, I could see every word the two men said, so long as they didn't turn away.

They did, of course, once in a while, and I had to piece together sentences where words got lost, but it made sense enough to make me realise that I'd really got into trouble this time.

The red-head was arguing, when I first got a hold on the conversation.

"Have a heart, Clint. He's only a nipper."

"And you're a mushy-hearted Aussie with bone between the ears, Blue," the fat man snapped back. He had unpleasantly thin lips, and he bit his words off as if he hated them. "He's fifteen, maybe sixteen years old. He's not a kid. You were a perishing idiot to bring him in here."

"What the 'ell d'you expect . . . leave him out in the proton storm? Have a heart, Clint."

"Heart? Yours'll get you into trouble. I tell you straight, there's no room in LEMCON for softies."

"LEMCON!" The red-head swore fluently for a full eighty seconds. "I tell you straight, Clint, I've never known anything . . . I've mined for opal in Andamooka at a hundred and eighty Fahrenheit, where the flies would tear living chunks outta you, if they didn't drive you bonkers first, that is . . . you couldn't trust the man next to you not to cut your throat and grab your swag while you slept . . . mining in the Rand the year the blacks rebelled, blood running like water in the adits . . . never such a Godforsaken rotten dump as this . . . so help me, when my contract's up you won't see me for dust."

"Nobody forced you here. You signed a free contract. The pay's the best in the Universe." The fat man's eyes stared coldly at me as he spoke. I lay still. The red-head moved restlessly.

"The *pay* . . . no pay good enough for a job . . . living in a 'ole like a bleeding mole, smelling your own sweat for eight hours straight in a perishing space-suit. No pubs. No women. No decent tucker for eighteen months."

"What do you mean — decent tucker? How often did you get your teeth into a genuine steak back on Earth, bucko?"

"'Aven't had steak for a week and you know it. Nothing but

34

tinned junk."

"Come off it! Supply ship had to bring all those extra drill bits up, and you know it. Steak'll be in next week."

The red-head rubbed his face. ". . . and overtime. Last week I put in eighty hours. I was bleeding near asleep in my feet."

"LEMCON's no place for softies." The thin lips smiled.

The red-head's arm came up, sinewy, tanned, and the fat man moved back. "Lay a hand on me, Aussie, and you're on report. You know the rules."

"Lay off name-calling then, or you're no cobber of mine. Anyway you need me to do your leg-work for you. Now tell me straight . . . what's going on? . . . tearing minerals out so fast you'd think we were trying to gut Moon . . . doesn't make sense with triple-pay overtime and all those broken drill-bits."

Clint smiled coldly. "Don't you watch the television? LEMCON's nearly through, and Miles Fargo's got his orders. We've got to gouge every scrap of ore out of Aristarchus before the UN team gets here."

The man called Blue rubbed his face again. ". . . about the watch-you-call-it?"

"The moritorium? Make me laugh! Fargo's got his orders. LEMCON is grabbing and getting out. With no water, oxides, cargo ships, where will the colonists be then? Five years, ten at the most, Moon will be abandoned. Then LEMCON can step back in and take over, the way it should have in the first place."

"That's dirty."

"So? Playing clean may win you Brownie points, but it isn't money in the bank, now is it?"

"All right. So why fuss about the boy? Once the UN team hits Imbrium Terminal they'll see right off what Fargo's been doing."

The fat man shrugged, his cold eyes still on me. I lay motionless on the narrow cot, one arm flung up, my head turned towards the door, eyes three parts shut. "You still don't get it, you dumb Aussie. If the UN doesn't suspect anything illegal they'll be in no hurry to get up here. By the time they've appointed a chairman and bickered over who should be represented on the team we'll have had a full year to clean up. Maybe more. A skirmish or two in

35

central Africa might distract them."

The Australian stared. "Miles Fargo could do *that?*"

"Fargo? Don't make me laugh! LEMCON is deeper and wider than Miles Fargo ever dreamed, Blue. There's more money than you could ever dream of wrapped up in this . . . petrodollars. Stick with me, Blue and you'll end up rich. But that kid saw the stockpiles, the number of excavators . . . he knows we've got the inhibitor. That's bad. We were warned. Now do you see what you did when you got all soft-hearted and dragged that boy in here?"

Silence. Then, "What'll we do, Clint?"

"Get rid of him of course."

I shut my eyes and swallowed, trying to bottle up the panic that was surging up in me. My forehead was wet and I couldn't breathe evenly any more.

I heard the door open, and kept my eyes shut. A hand was suddenly hard on my shoulder, shaking me. I groaned and rolled over on to my back, blinking up at the two men who stood over me, as if I'd just seen them for the first time.

"On your feet," the fat man snapped. His voice was softer than I'd expected, almost a whisper, deep in his fat throat. I swung my feet off the cot and looked round. The small white room was empty except for the bed. The room beyond seemed to be furnished as an office, with a desk, chairs, and a couple of cabinets. The door beyond was shut.

"Your name? Where are you from?" The soft voice persisted.

"Kepler . . ." I began to stammer, my mind twisting this way and that for an escape. Then it hit me. The cosmic storm must have cut communications. There could have been no frantic enquiries for Kepler Masterman, son of Moon Governor. . . . If I could just make Clint and Blue believe I was nobody important, that it was all a mistake, then maybe, just maybe, they'd let me go.

"I'm from Kepler Base," I went on. I had hesitated only for a second or two. "My name's Eric Erickson."

"Who's your father?"

"Bjorn Erickson, sir. Astronomer."

"Why are you here? You know LEMCON property's off-limits to you colonists."

36

"Yes, sir. I'm sorry. I didn't mean to . . ." I let my voice trail off.

"Don't call me sir. I'm not one of your fancy colonists. Kepler Base is four hundred miles away. You couldn't have got here by mistake. The truth, now!"

So I told them the truth, about the party and riding the terminal.

"Parties?" The fat man sneered. "Spoiled kids! At your age I'd been scrounging my bread for a couple of years. Well, it's stupid enough to be true. You'd better hope it is." He turned to the red-headed man. "Watch him, Blue, while I check this out."

He left the room, moving lightly for a fat man. I caught a glimpse of a white-painted corridor just before the door slammed. I stood up and looked at the room beyond. It was an office, stark and functional. There were no view screens, nothing to give me a clue as to where under Aristarchus I was.

As a prison it was perfect. Even if I could find my way up to the air-locks I had no idea what had happened to my moon-suit or the crawler. Without them I was tied hands and feet. The fat man must have known that. Yet he'd told Blue to guard me. Why?

I'd better find out fast. It would only be a matter of hours before communications cleared up and the LEMCON men found out who I really was, and I had the sure and certain feeling that being the son of Moon Governor was not going to be an asset this time.

I felt suddenly giddy and clutched at the door frame with a hand that was slippery with sweat. I gulped.

"You all right, boy?" Blue spoke with a strong Australian twang.

"Yes, I think . . ." I sat down abruptly on the cot. The sick feeling wore off and my mind, turning this way and that like a trapped animal, began to improvise. "The radiation . . . was I outside long?"

"Nah." His voice was comforting. "Not to worry. I got you in a good ten minutes before the storm hit."

"I don't understand. I passed out . . . I remember trying to get my crawler up the slope to the crater top. But that's all. Did you find me up near the rim? How did you see me?"

Blue looked puzzled and I could see him searching for an answer. "Your carbon dioxide scrubbers couldn't have been

37

working properly," he said slowly after a long pause. "The air was pretty bad when I got you out. You don't remember?"

"Remember what?"

"You were right down on the crater floor near our air-locks. You don't remember getting there?"

I shook my head. Blue was still staring at me when Clint came back. He spoke to Blue as if I wasn't there. "There *is* an Eric Erickson. Fifteen years old. Been on Kepler Base for three years."

"No, five," I interrupted. The Ericksons had come up to Moon on the same ferry as Ann and her family, so I was sure. Out of the corner of my eye I saw the fat man relax ever so slightly. He nodded to Blue, just the faintest movement of his head.

I let my breath out very slowly. It looked as if I had been reprieved, for the moment anyway.

Blue stretched his bony height from the door frame where he'd been leaning. "Hungry, boy? Could you use some tucker?"

"Thank you, sir. I *am* hungry. Starving, actually."

"Good on you." He lounged from the room.

The fat man stared at me with his marble cold eyes. I stood defensively and stared back.

"Starving? I thought you told me you kids had been having a party?" He smiled and two dimples appeared in his pink cheeks. The contrast between his cold eyes and the dimples was horrible. I felt as if I'd just seen a corpse smile. The skin on the back of my neck crawled. I dropped my eyes and stared at the floor.

"It wasn't that kind of party," I muttered. "Just music and dancing and yeast-culture biscuits for the little ones."

He didn't say anything and after a while the silence became unbearable. "I suppose you think it's pretty stupid our having New Day parties, but . . . well, it gives some sort of shape to the year, and the small kids love it." I chattered on desperately.

"Uh-huh."

"I suppose you don't go in for that sort of thing over here? . . . celebrations, I mean."

"We work. We eat. We sleep. That's it."

"But surely there must be enough of you to make get-togethers worth while. Music, plays, something. Do you all live alone and

38

eat separately, like this?"

"What are you asking questions for? Why do you want to know?"

"I'm sorry, sir. I didn't mean . . . no special reason."

I was thankful that Blue came in at that moment, with a tray which he dumped on the table. "There you are, chum. Let's see you get outside that."

Clint was standing between me and the table. I hesitated and then tried to walk around him. He reached out and grabbed my arm. He may have looked flabby, but he wasn't. Under the fat was steel. I could feel the grip of each separate finger for the next hour. "No special reason, eh?" He pushed me away roughly. "Watch him, Blue." His cold eyes looked at the Australian. Then he left the room again.

I stared after him, rubbing my arm. Then the smell of hot food came drifting to me off the tray and I sat down at the table and waded in.

Blue watched me curiously. "When did you last eat a meal like that?" he asked.

"Not since I was on Earth," I said with my mouth full of hot gravy and potatoes.

"Five years ago? That's a long time between meals. You don't look starved."

I remembered who I was supposed to be just in time to stop myself from telling him that I'd been back on Moon for less than a month. I choked and took a hasty swig of water, fresh again, none of our re-cycled stuff.

"We mostly eat synthetic food," I volunteered. "It's very nourishing, but it certainly doesn't taste like much and you can get awfully tired of it after a while. This is marvellous."

"Marvellous? It's only canned stew, mate, not pheasant under glass."

"*Canned* stew? But that's a punishing pay-load in cargo-weight calories. How on Moon do you get it *up* here?"

It was his turn to stare. "By ore carrier, of course. They go down to Earth full, and they'd come back empty, except for our supplies. LEMCON wouldn't get experienced miners up here if it wasn't for

39

good food. Miners are choosy about their tucker."

I mulled over this as I ate. "But if the ore carriers are coming back to Moon half empty, why can't the colonists get supplies from Earth too?"

He shrugged. "I suppose you could if you cared to pay for them."

"Do you have any idea how much LEMCON charges us for Earth freight?"

"Whatever the traffic can bear, I suppose. They're not in this just for love, you know."

"It's not fair, sir. It really isn't fair." I pushed my plate away. "The colonists were here first. They were here for fifteen years before LEMCON got the mining charter. It was their Moon technology that made the mines a paying proposition."

"Sure, boy, sure. But look at what LEMCON's given you in return. Fair's fair. And stop calling me sir. Me name's Blue."

"Yes, sir . . . Blue. Well, what has LEMCON given us? You charge us so much for water that it has to be rationed and re-cycled. And after we've paid Earth rates for the oxides we need there's no money left for fancy food or nice furniture or anything like that. We live in uniforms and our homes are like army barracks. We eat cultured food and pay through the nose for every extra. And not a cent in royalties from LEMCON. Why, that's what the UN Mandate is all about."

Blue didn't answer me for a moment. Then he laughed. "Well, I must say you do it well. They've certainly got you young ones indoctrinated, haven't they? Oh, don't look so innocent. That's propaganda talk. Everyone knows you colonists have it easy, living in nice homes with your wives and kiddies, working clean and comfortable. What do you think it's like for us, eh? Mucking it on top under the blazing sun or the freezing night for eighteen blinking months, with nothing to come home to but an empty room. What do you think it feels like?"

"Why do you do it then? Why did you come here?"

"I must have been barmy, I think. It was the money, of course. What other reason would anyone but a nut have for coming to Moon?"

"But that's no . . ."

The door burst open and the fat man was there. He grabbed me with one huge paw and slapped me across the face with the other. My head snapped back. I struggled and he hit me again. And again. My knees sagged and I slumped against him.

Blue grabbed him and tore him off me. "What the 'ell are you doing, Clint?"

I collapsed into a chair.

"The little twister. I'll give it to him."

"Cool down a bit and let me in on it. What's he done? He sounds harmless enough to me. Full of nonsense, but harmless."

"*Harmless*. That's a laugh! He's been lying, Blue, lying like a pro. He's not Eric Erickson. The radio's working again. There's no Erickson missing from Kepler Base."

"So? Maybe they're sloppy. Maybe they just haven't missed him yet, that's all. You think of that before you started hitting?"

"There *is* a crawler missing, Blue. *And* a kid with it. Only it's no astronomer's brat. It's the Governor's own kid, Kepler Masterman. That's who we've got here, nosing around Aristarchus. It's the Moon Governor's brat!"

"Cor!" Blue stared at me and then laughed uncertainly. "I knew it was all just propaganda, what you were spouting. I thought as much."

"It wasn't, Blue. It was true, all of it. I just didn't want to tell you my real name in case I got into more trouble, that's all. But what I told you was true, honestly. Why don't you take me back to Kepler Base and you can see for yourself. My father would show you around. Then you could decide who's in the right, us or LEMCON."

"You been listening to him, Blue?" Clint smiled coldly. "You always were soft in the head. You'd better start listening to me for a change, or I'll have to start looking around for another partner."

"Are you threatening me?"

"Just telling. Now shut up. I've got to think. Did anyone see you bring him in, anyone at all?"

Blue shook his head.

"Good. Then if we can get him out of here unnoticed we can

41

arrange for him to have a little accident about half way back to Kepler. That way LEMCON won't even come into it."

"What kind of accident?"

"I haven't worked out the details yet. Be quiet, Blue."

"I won't stand for murder, Clint. Not a kid. And there's no need, I tell you. He hasn't seen a thing, not a bloody thing."

"What do you mean?"

He glanced at me and lowered his voice. "The inhibitor, Clint. He don't remember a thing, straight. There's no need to put him away."

"He's a spy."

"Go on, Clint. You've got spies on the brain. It doesn't make sense. Why don't you just turn him over to the boss, if you're worried?"

"To Fargo? Make me laugh! Fargo would just hand him over to his daddy, as mild as milk. I'm not answerable to Fargo, Blue, and I'll tell you straight, the men I *do* work for would want this kid out of the way for good. And they'd be very unhappy with you if I were to tell them that it was your idiocy that made getting rid of him necessary."

The tan on the Australian's face seemed to fade. "What d'you mean? Hey, leave me out of it."

"Not likely. You're in it, Blue, all the way. And what's turned *you* so milky all of a sudden? Are you forgetting that I know all about that man you clobbered at Andamooka back in '97?"

"That was different, and you know it. He had it coming. He stole me hoard of opals that took me four months of flaming hell to mine. And he wasn't just a kid either."

"They're cunning, these colonists, really crafty. I reckon they figured you'd think that way. Reckon that's why they sent a kid to spy on us. And now you want us to escort him back to Kepler Base, nice and polite, and hand him over to his daddy, the Governor. Then he tells his daddy just how many excavators he saw here, the ore stock-piles, and his daddy calls the UN. Before you can holler 'uncle' there's a swarm of UN observers all over Aristarchus. Then you'll be out of a job, Blue, and not just on Moon. Because when we get back to Earth I'll see you're boycotted. You'll never get another job where my friends have influence, and believe me, Blue, that's everywhere. And it'll all be this kid's fault, Blue, just as much as if he stole the bonus right out of your pocket."

"But if he saw nothing, Clint?"

"No, Blue. There's still the inhibitor field. He'll be bound to talk about it and then we'll be in big trouble. Use your head. We've got to get rid of him. Think about it, Blue. He's no different from the guy that stole your opals."

I watched the Australian's face change and harden. Five minutes earlier Blue was almost a friend. Now he looked at me as if he really hated me. Nothing at all had really changed. Only quite suddenly they were two against one.

Chapter Five

HOW DO YOU RUN, when there's nowhere to run to? I had no
moon-suit. I didn't know what Blue had done with my crawler. I
hadn't the faintest idea of the layout of the Aristarchus complex,
how far underground I was, where the elevators were, how the
locks worked. Then there was that thing called the "Inhibitor".
Whatever it was, it hadn't done me any good coming *in*, and I had
the sinking feeling that it would probably be just as bad for anyone
trying to get *out*.

So when Blue looked at me with eyes that had flashes of anger in
them like the fire in his Australian opals, and Clint said, "Come
on, kid, and no fuss," I stood up meekly and went with them out of
the room.

From down the corridor came a burst of raucous laughter. For a
split second I hesitated. Would Clint dare to kill me right in the
heart of LEMCON's complex? If I could just get to those other miners
. . . two people might conspire to murder, but surely not ten or
twenty. It *was* only those two, I suddenly realised. That's why they
had watched me so closely. I didn't have to get *out* of Aristarchus,
just away from Clint and Blue. As a businessman, Miles Fargo
might be as crooked as Schröter's Valley, but he wasn't a criminal
. . . if I could get to him.

I doubled back between the two men and pelted down that long
white corridor. My hand was on the door knob. I could hear
voices and the sound of laughter. I opened my mouth to yell.

A leather-hard hand came down over it, and steel fingers bit into
my upper arm. I was turned and pushed, struggling, back along the
corridor, and into the elevator.

The door slid shut between us and the sound of ordinary human beings, and we began to move upward. "Just try that again . . ." Clint opened his hand and showed me a gun, a nasty-looking Earth weapon. I'd never actually seen one before, but I'd read what they could do.

I gulped and shook my head. "I won't. I promise."

The doors opened to show another corridor, white-painted, undecorated, running to left and right, with a number of branches at each end, like the fingers on a hand.

We turned to the right and walked briskly along, Blue ahead, the fat man just behind me, the gun hard in my ribs. From one of the terminal passages a group of men suddenly appeared and came towards us. Clint's stride didn't even break, but I felt the gun jab painfully into my ribs.

He needn't have worried. The men pushed past us unseeingly. They were unshaven, smelling of sweat, dazed with fatigue. One of them lurched against me in the narrow corridor and for an instant we were face to face. I could smell the bitter moon-dust on his clothes, and see where the sweat had dried in runnels down his forehead and cheeks. There was something odd about his eyes, and a scar ran puckered and white from the corner of one eye to his cheekbone.

Before I even had time to react he had pushed past me, indifferent, unseeing. I had the feeling that even if I could have broken away from Clint and Blue, even if I had run back after the men, they wouldn't have understood or even heard me. In a few seconds they were all gone, swallowed up by the elevators, and the three of us were alone again.

"That was wise," Clint said softly, and the pressure of the gun relaxed. We paused at the end of the main corridor. Now I could see that each of the branches was lined with change lockers, and that the door at the far end of each passage was an air-lock entrance.

We turned down the extreme right hand branch, and Clint opened a locker and pushed a clumsy Earth-type space-suit into my arms.

"Put it on, kid. Look sharp about it."

The sheer weight of it in my arms made my knees sag. "I can't

45

wear this thing," I protested. "It's far too big and heavy."

"You'll do as you're told." Clint's arm came up, but as I ducked Blue grabbed him.

"Hold on, Clint. The kid's right. We don't want him *found* in one of our suits, do we?"

Clint's arm dropped and he smiled. The dimples in his fat cheeks deepened. "That's good, Blue. You're learning. All right. What did you do with the kid's suit? Hurry up. We don't want him seen."

"It's in me locker. Hang on. Here it is. I shoved it in behind me gear. Flimsy sort of thing, isn't it? I wouldn't want to trust myself in one of these." He tossed it to me.

"Well, it won't have to do him that long." The fat man smiled, and the look in his eyes sent a finger of space-cold down my spine. I had checked the seal of my helmet and gauntlets, and my oxygen pack and carbon dioxide scrubber, before they had finished struggling into their heavy old-fashioned suits.

Clint punched the wall-button marked "ATM". I could hear the air-pump inside the lock. The red light went out and the green atmosphere indicator came on. The hatch slid open before the two had finished suiting up.

"Come on." Clint glanced down the corridor. "In you go." As the hatch slid shut behind us I could see that the corridor was still empty. Nobody in Aristarchus had seen me, except these two and the miners punch-drunk with fatigue coming off shift.

The luck had all gone their way so far. I was due for a break, and I'd better be on my toes when it came. I watched Blue and Clint check out each other's suit, not just once but twice. They were afraid, I realised. They were afraid of Moon. By insulating themselves from her in their clumsy old-style space-suits, they'd come to see Moon as the enemy.

I remembered my first experience SCUBA diving down on Conshelf Ten, the wonderful sense of freedom that the light-weight wet-suit and the back pack of compressed air had given me. Our moon-suits gave us the same kind of freedom.

LEMCON had turned its back on Moon colony and on everything we stood for, including our advanced Moon technology, and now

46

they had to pay the price for rejecting knowledge. They were not at home and I was.

I watched them as the air pumped out of the lock. There were two of them, each nearly twice my weight. But I belonged here. Moon was *my* planet. I had been born under its gravity and I was no stranger to vacuum. I could read the position of the Sun and Earth and the stars, and reckon to within a few miles exactly where I was, night or day, as easily as a child on Earth might find its way home from kindergarten.

And I was not afraid of Moon. That was my most important weapon. I was like a guerrilla fighter against two thugs in medi-aeval armour. If I could wait for exactly the right moment I figured I stood a better than even chance . . . if that moment came . . . if I recognised it when it did. . . .

The pumps stopped and the outer door slid open to Moon space. The lock was built below grade and we had to walk up a sloping ramp caked with moon-dust to the surface. How many hours had I been below?

It couldn't have been long. The floor of the crater was dotted with work-lights and the head-lamps of mining vehicles, but the sun was still below the crater rim. I only had time for a fast glance around, and then I was being jostled across a compound towards a huddle of vehicles. My crawler was there, hidden among them. On my own I could never have found it. I tried to slow down my movements to the men's clumsy plod. The less they knew about my capabilities the better the element of surprise, if and when I had the chance.

Clint put his helmet against Blue's so that he could talk directly to him without using the suit intercom to which anyone around might listen in. Since the vacuum of moon space can't carry sound I couldn't hear a word he said. But that didn't matter. He was standing below and to one side of a cluster of work lights, and the light shone through the lower part of his visor. His eyes were in shadow, but I could see his lips clearly. I could see every word. . . .

"I'll go with the kid in his crawler, Blue. You follow close be-hind and keep in our tracks. Mind you don't lose us, now. When we're safely away from Aristarchus I'll crack open his lock and join you. We'll be back here long before they find him. There's no way they'll ever be able to prove it was anything but his own carelessness."

Blue's helmet nodded a slow acknowledgment. His face was shadowed so I had no idea what he was thinking. If he had been the one to pilot my crawler, maybe I could have talked some sense into him . . . but of course Clint knew that. That was why the fat man was coming with me.

Clint and I boarded my crawler and crossed the floor of Aristarchus without incident. Whatever the inhibitor was, it didn't seem to be working now. We hair-pinned up the track to the crater rim and tipped down the outer slope towards the surface of the *mare*. It was black night out there, as far as the horizon, almost thirty miles away from the height of the crater rim.

Once down on the *mare* Clint cast about, to-ing and fro-ing, as if he was looking for something. He saw it in the same instant I did, the tracks of my crawler, compacted in moon-dust, leading away from all the other vehicle tracks, straight as a comet trail, back to Kepler Base.

The lights of the crawler, slung low on its chassis, threw the distinctive design of the treads into high relief. Not a grain of dust had moved since I had been by. With no rain or wind to disturb them they might remain like that, mint new, for a thousand years. Obviously Clint didn't want that.

He was a bad man, was Clint, and his very presence raised goose bumps on my skin, but he was one of the best drivers I had ever seen. He could never have driven a moon crawler before, but within a few minutes he had got the hang of the controls. Now he drove the crawler back along its own tracks.

Looking over my shoulder I could see the wide-tracked mining vehicle that Blue was driving. It was so close behind us that its head lights illuminated the dust kicked up by our treads, and for a moment there was an illusion of atmosphere as the dust hung in a foggy patch between us and the other's headlights.

By the time he had crisscrossed our tracks all the way out and all the way back who would be able to say how many vehicles had gone this way, and when. How many miles would they back-track over my trail towards Kepler, I wondered, before it was time for me to die? I tried to keep my breathing even and my mind clear as I waited, waited and watched for Clint to make a mistake.

We were nearly a hundred miles out from Aristarchus before the moment I had been waiting for came. The sun was still below the horizon to our left. On Moon there was no pre-dawn light, no red flush in the eastern sky. But I saw, and knew Clint would never notice, the first faint pearly flicker of the sun's corona.

In less than a minute its blinding light would flare out across the flat surface of the *mare* and strike the dusty bubble of the crawler. Within fifteen seconds the glass would darken in response to the light stimulus, but for that precious fifteen seconds we would be virtually driving blind.

Desperately I scanned the surface directly ahead of the crawler for something I could use as a diversion. In a few seconds. . . . It was all a matter of timing. One second too early and he would see what I was up to. One second too late and he'd have slowed down in response to the sun dazzle.

It was there, just to our right. Exactly what I needed. If Clint had been concentrating on anything except keeping in my tracks he'd have noticed why I had swerved on the trip to Aristarchus, to avoid the big dust boil. I watched the horizon, my muscles tensed.

A flare of light shot out from the eastern sky like an arrow of pure energy, and struck the curved plexiglass of the crawler bubble. From across the cabin I vaulted, feather-light in my moon suit.

"Look out, man! Don't you see it? Turn!" I screamed and yanked the steering wheel hard over to the right.

The wheel spun under my hand as Clint, sun-blinded, put his left arm up to shield his eyes. The element of surprise had worked perfectly. Before he could grip the wheel again I felt the crawler crunch on the unstable edge of the boil. It hesitated for a breath-taking second and then settled, floundering and whining in the dust.

The whole thing could have taken no more than ten seconds, and the fat man had barely time to register what had happened before it was all over. He swore and stamped on the accelerator. The treads bit deep into the dust, churning it up around us. The crawler settled deeper. The jets choked, overheated and died.

We sat in silence while slowly, very slowly, the dust began to settle. In a couple of minutes I could see the LEMCON vehicle, Blue peering anxiously through its screen. He'd pulled up abreast of us, over to the left, on firm ground.

"What is it? What did you do?" Clint's voice was sharp with suspicion.

"You didn't see it?" I acted amazed. "Boy, it's one of the worst I've met. I tried to yell at you to stop, but there wasn't enough time."

"What is it?" He pushed his face at me.

"A dust boil," I answered truthfully.

"What the hell's *that*?"

"Oh, it's where, a long time ago, a bubble of gas escaped from inside the Moon. It left a thin porous crust, like a soap film. In time that broke down and it slowly filled with dust. It might take a million years to make one this full of dust. Some are even bigger, big enough to swallow a whole crawler, right over its roof."

That bit was a lie, but it was effective. He was beginning to sweat. I could see beads of moisture running down his forehead under his heavy helmet. "How do you get out of these things? You *can* get out?"

"I don't know. Maybe." I made my voice tremble. "But it's not going to be easy. You have to have another vehicle to winch you out. That's why we ordinarily travel in pairs. Though dust boils are usually easy to see and avoid. It was just bad luck hitting this one right at sun-rise."

"We're not too deep in? We're not trapped? The locks will still work, eh?"

His mind was working just the way I'd hoped it would. It was hard for me to keep the smile out of my voice. "Oh, yes, sir. This one isn't *that* deep. Maybe a foot, eighteen inches. But we probably won't have to lock out. If your friend Blue will just get in behind us with a cable he'll be able to winch us right out of here."

Clint sat silently for a moment and then began to chuckle. It was a grisly sound. "So you always travel in pairs, do you? It's too bad you forgot that rule when you went joy-riding up the terminator, isn't it, Kepler Masterman? By yourself you'd be completely helpless, wouldn't you? You'd just sit here until you ran out of air. Or you could walk, of course . . ." He chuckled again.

I mustn't be too quick. He didn't know I'd read his lips. "But we're not by ourselves. Blue can . . ."

"Oh, Blue can't help you, I'm afraid. No, he wouldn't have any idea how to go about it. After all, he's only a stranger on Moon, isn't he?"

I stared at him, and let my mouth fall open. Then I stammered. "But you're here, too. It's your air that'll run out as well as mine. Tell him he's got to help us. Make him . . ."

"Oh, I couldn't do that. Independent fellow, Blue is. But don't concern yourself with me. I'll be all right. You see I've got somewhere to go." He stood up. "And look at it this way, kid. When I'm gone your oxygen will last twice as long, won't it? Really I'm doing you a favour."

I clung to his legs and screamed. "You can't leave me here, I'll die. Nobody'll come this way for years. I'll die. And it's murder." I put everything I'd got into my terror.

He kicked me aside with his weighted boot. "You shouldn't have interfered, kid. When LEMCON says a place is out of bounds, then that's the way it is."

"But I couldn't help it. I didn't mean to . . ."

"I've got my orders, boy." He pushed past me and disabled the radio with one quick yank.

"If you abandon me here, it's murder. You'll never get off Moon. They'll find you."

He shook his head. "Murder? No, not this time. Only an unfortunate accident. Nobody'll ask questions. I'll shut the air-lock and pressurise it behind me. It's all turned out very neat. I couldn't have planned it better myself."

He fastened his visor and pushed past me into the air-lock. I let him go. It was no part of my plan to be knocked unconscious in a final struggle.

The air hissed out of the lock. I heard the outer hatch open and

51

then close again. The pumps restarted. Clint pounded the outside of the crawler with his fist in a triumphant farewell.

I peered through the dust-covered bubble and saw him wallow out of the dust boil and clump over to the LEMCON vehicle. The airlock opened to admit him. In another minute it had backed up, turned and moved off. Two minutes later and two miles away and it was out of sight.

I was alone. I let out a long shaky breath and got down to work.

What Clint couldn't possibly have known, and what I, of course, wasn't about to tell him, was that crawlers, in fact all our vehicles, come equipped with a fine array of safety devices to get one out of just the sort of jam I was in now.

The jets were deep in choking dust. I couldn't risk using them in case I blew the whole crawler apart. I'd have to get out on batteries alone. We were in this particular boil pretty deep, and Clint gunning the motor at the last minute like that hadn't helped.

I checked the temperature and started the battery engines. They caught right away. It was lucky for me that the dust in the boil was cold with the cold of two weeks of night. Then I started the auxiliary motor that operated a jack mounted permanently beneath the crawler. The motor whined and the front end of the crawler pushed slowly up out of the dust. I pulled a lever set among the driving controls and a grapnel shot out of its housing in the front of the crawler just above the wheels. It fell in the dust ten feet ahead, scratched a trail and retracted. I tried again. And again. The fourth time it caught in solid rock and held fast.

Slowly I started forward, concentrating on keeping the cable taut without snapping it, and retracting the jack as the cable took the strain. With infinite care I eased the crawler forward, up along the cable and out of the dust boil. The grapnel came loose and snapped back into its housing just as I came up on to level ground. I gunned the motors and fired my rear jets all at the same time, and the crawler half wallowed, half blew, on to firm ground.

I sat still for a moment, with my hands shaking and my mouth as dry as the moon-dust that hung in a cloud above the crawler. Then, while I waited for the dust to clear, I got up from the driver's seat. My knees were wobbling most unaccountably, I noticed. I dug out the emergency supplies and took a protein pill and a swig of tepid, re-cycled water. Then I glanced over at my oxygen supply indicator and sat down to set a course back to Kepler Base.

I followed my tracks all the way, and I must have broken every record in the book for crawler speed. I made the lock entrance at Kepler with five minutes oxygen to spare, so at least the safety patrol didn't have to come out and haul me in.

They were there waiting for me, though, when I cracked the air-lock into the dome, and walked out, all stiff-legged and wobbly. They escorted me down to my sleep cubicle on the third floor. The rest of "A" watch was on duty, and the whole wing was deserted. So to add to my other sins I'd also missed a duty watch.

"I've got to talk to my father," I begged them. "There's something I just have to tell him. It's important."

But they only shook their heads and shut the door on me.

I sat on the edge of my narrow bed and worried. Then I walked up and down the room. Four paces one way. Four the other. I'd like to have had a good wash, but I didn't want to open the door to the corridor and maybe find a guard there, as if I really was a criminal. I didn't want to know if that was how bad it was. So in the end I settled for changing into a clean uniform and tidying my hair. Then I paced some more.

Finally the door opened. "The Governor will see you now."

Not "your father" . . . "The Governor".

I swallowed and walked past the man to the elevators. On Admin floor I could feel everyone's eyes on me, and I went through to Father's office with my cheeks and ears flaming.

Chapter Six

I HAD HARDLY SEEN anything of Father since we had got back from Earth three weeks before. He looked older and very tired, and he seemed to have lost some of the springiness that had always seemed so much a part of him. Did I do that? I wondered. I found myself being angry with him and ashamed of myself all at the same time.

"Kepler, why?," was all he said, but the look that accompanied the question knocked everything about Aristarchus and LEMCON out of my head. I found myself shrugging helplessly.

"Come on, Kep. Sit down. Tommy, no calls or visitors, please," he called to his secretary, and then shut the door. "Kep, why did you do it?" he asked again. His voice was very gentle.

"I don't know. I really don't. I just . . . I'm sorry, Father."

"What's gone wrong? Ever since we got back from Earth I've been hearing disturbing reports about you."

My chin went up at that. "From Ann's father, I suppose?"

"Well, you certainly seem to have gone out of your way to upset Ann. You must know that even better than I do. But I've heard from your teachers. Your fellow-students. If I didn't know you better I'd be tempted to think that being a hero down on Earth had gone to your head."

"That's not fair!" The suggestion really stung me. If I had been thinking about Earth and Conshelf Ten rather a lot recently it was about the friends I'd made down there and not the hero stuff. "It's not that at all!" I jumped up so hastily that I knocked the chair over. "Sorry. It's not that, Father. It's . . . oh, it's hard to put into words . . . it's just, well, Moon doesn't seem to be the way it was any more. Everyone is so serious. Nobody seems to have time for fun or . . . or play, or . . "

"Some people who come up here to observe call it dedication. You used to be that way yourself, Kep. I don't think we've changed. It's just that it never bothered you before. I wonder why it does now?"

"Maybe because I'd never seen anything else. Because I never knew life could be different from the way it is up here. Down on Earth there are so many more choices, so much freedom."

"'How are you going to keep them down on the farm, after they've seen Paree?'" Father quoted.

"Huh?"

"Just a very old song, from one of Earth wars, about the effects of tasting freedom and glamour. Kep, did you ever stop to consider that all the adults here, and most of the children, have come from Earth, have turned their back on all these choices and freedoms you think are so important, in order to help make Moon colony grow? They think they've found something much better up here."

"But it was their choice, Father. I'm not saying they were wrong and I was right. But they all had the chance of making that choice and I didn't. I got born up here, and I'm stuck with it."

"And not having that freedom bothers you."

"I guess it does. Yes."

"Very well, Kepler. It's yours."

I must have just looked blank.

"The choice. It's yours," he repeated. "Do you want to stay with Moon and commit your future together with us who believe in Moon? Or would you rather go back to Earth? You may, if you choose. I can arrange it."

It was the funniest thing. As soon as Father gave me the choice I found that I didn't want it that badly after all. My mind raced around inside itself thinking of plausible reasons for not giving up on Moon colony. The strongest, the one that kept coming back to my mind, was the picture of Hilary's face if I were to turn my back on Moon's troubles and go back to Conshelf Ten. Hilary could never stand a quitter. But that reason was too personal to discuss with Father.

I opened my mouth and shut it again. Then, "Can I think about it, Father?" I asked cautiously.

I thought he looked disappointed, but I wasn't sure. It was only a flash. Then he smiled and said briskly, "Yes, of course. It's not the sort of decision you can make in a moment. Take your time. Think about it and let me know."

There was an awkward pause. Then he put the tips of his fingers together in the way he always did when he was arbitrating a decision. He frowned, and looked across his desk at me over the top of them. "I appreciate that it has been difficult for you to adjust, Kepler, and I really regret that I haven't had more time to talk with you, to be available when you needed me . . ."

"I do understand, Father," I put in.

"*But*," he went on as if I hadn't spoken. "Your most recent exploit is inexcusable. To take a crawler. To go out alone. To ignore radio signals and storm warnings. Any one of these violations could have got you killed. You of all people, brought up in the understanding of the necessity of all these regulations . . . I still can't understand how you got back here safely, where you were when . . ."

"I went to Aristarchus," I interrupted.

"You did what!" It was like seeing the peaceful *mare* suddenly erupt into a flaming volcano. Then he calmed himself with a visible effort and sat down again. I could *hear* the silence in the big office outside. Even the typewriters had stopped.

"You'd better tell me about it," he said drily, after the silence had become almost unbearable.

I told him the whole story, holding nothing back. He didn't move or interrupt. His expression didn't change, even when I told him how I'd seen and heard how LEMCON was disregarding the UN's ban on further mining operations. Only when I told him how Clint had planned my death did I see how his hand clenched until the knuckles whitened.

There was another long silence after I'd finished. "So that's it," I added feebly, after the silence got too painful. "I really am sorry, Father."

"All right," he said absently. I had the disconcerting feeling that

56

his mind was light-years away and that he wasn't thinking about me at all. Then he blinked and stared at me as he might have stared at a witness in court, as if I wasn't his son at all. It was a very odd feeling, and I didn't much like it.

"I want you to go through your whole story again," he said. "This time for the recorder. Start from where you approached Aristarchus, and make sure you leave nothing out, absolutely nothing."

I went through it again, and then a third time, with questions.

"You're quite sure there was nothing wrong with your scrubber?"

"Blue called that field an *inhibitor*?"

"Tell me again what Clint said when Blue asked if he were personally employed by Miles Fargo?"

And on, and on, until my head ached and my nerves were snapping raw.

Then he suddenly stood up. "Very well, Kepler. Now I want your word that nothing, absolutely nothing, that you've told me, goes outside this room. Do I have it?"

I shrugged. "Yes, sir. I suppose so. But . . ."

"No buts about it. It's absolutely vital. Do I have your word?"

"Suppose people ask me where I've been? Suppose Ann . . ."

"You'll say nothing at all. Is that completely clear?"

"Yes, sir, it's clear. Father, What is the inhibitor? And why weren't you even surprised when I told you how LEMCON was robbing Moon? When I looked for you last week Tommy said you were in Aristarchus, but you couldn't have been. Where were you? Father, what's going on?"

For a moment he hesitated, and then shook his head.

I swallowed. "I suppose you can't trust me, after what I did."

"I didn't say that, Kepler."

"You didn't have to. Will you ever forget it? It was a mistake. I'm sorry. I won't do it again."

"You're lucky you have the chance to make that decision. Moon doesn't usually give second chances." He looked at me, and for a moment his expression softened to a smile. Then his face became stern again. He stood erect behind his desk. Moon Governor,

57

I suddenly remembered, was Judge as well as Governor for the whole colony. "For taking a crawler and for disobeying safety regulations you're grounded till next dawn."

"Yes, sir."

"You may go now, Kepler."

"Yes, *sir*!" I stormed out of the office, and only just stopped myself from slamming the door when I saw Tommy's scandalised expression. It's not that I was angry at the punishment. Father was better than fair. It could have been much more severe. The rest of the lunar day, twenty-seven Earth days long, was time enough to be without recreation privileges, or the chance to leave the Base even for a five minute Moon walk, but Father would have been completely justified in penalising me far more severely than that. I knew it, and he knew that I knew it.

No, I was angry at him for keeping me in the dark. Something was going on. Something big that was like a shadow between us. Something secret, complex, vitally important. Something he wouldn't trust his own son with. And oh, how I hated him for not trusting me.

I worked off the watches one by one. I fought through that matrix theory, and I mastered all the computer circuits. I caught up with every page of the work I'd missed when I was down on Earth. I didn't criticise the Base once, or compare it unfavourably to Earth, at least not out loud. I was so good it was almost unbearable. And all the time I was burning inside.

When Ann came up to me in the cafeteria fifteen watches later, shortly after the dusk terminator had passed over the Base and we were into night again, I could have fallen on her neck with joy. Talking to her would get my mind off Father. I jumped up to pull out a chair for her and brought over a couple of mugs of coffee-substitute.

She started talking right away. "Kep, you've just got to help me."

She hadn't said one single word, even "sorry", since she'd left the dome at sun-rise and I'd gone joy-riding up the terminator. She hadn't even said she was glad to see me safely back, I realised, suddenly aggrieved.

That was the first thing she said: "Kep, you've got to help me. I don't know what to do. Daddy's disappeared. Nobody'll tell me where he is or what's happened. Kep, please help me."

I stared blankly at her across the cafeteria table. I had just finished breakfast and had a pile of books beside me ready for class. It was a quarter to eight. And Ann was on 'B' watch, I remembered. "What on Moon are you doing up here? You're supposed to be asleep," I pointed out.

"How can I sleep when something's happened to Daddy?" She sounded almost hysterical.

It was so unlike Ann that I pulled myself together and tried to forget my own worries. Her pale face looked even paler than usual, and her dark eyes were even darker. Her usually glossy hair was, well, not untidy, but not as smooth as usual. It was all most peculiar. I stared at her.

She stretched her hand out across the table and touched my arm. "Please help me, Kep. I've no one else to turn to."

"What about Guy Roget?" I couldn't resist the dig.

She had the grace to blush. "Oh, Kep, don't be so silly. You know he was just an excuse. I needed to get away from you, that's all."

I decided to let that pass.

"I'll do anything I can, Ann. You know that. But tell me quickly. I've got a lab in fifteen minutes."

"You could skip it, couldn't you? Just this once." I stared at her. There she went again, not sounding like Ann at all. More like me, really.

"Ann, I've only got twelve penalty watches to go. I don't want anyone reporting me for skipping classes. If we're going to talk it'll have to be somewhere else."

"We could go up to one of the study rooms in the library," she suggested, and got up and headed for the door before I'd even let her know that I would skip classes. Dr Sheppard disappeared? What on Moon was she talking about? I picked up my books and followed her. Well, there went my perfect record.

I found her in one of the sound-proof cubicles off the main library. I made her sit down. She had this tendency to pace up and down twisting her fingers together in a distracted way.

"Now go on, Ann. And start at the beginning."

"Well, it all began at the New Day party. After you went off in the crawler I was really upset. Well, you know, you'd been so odd ever since you got back from Earth."

"Odd?" I interrupted. "What on Moon do you mean by that? I'd just started seeing things the way they really are up here, that's all."

"Well, never mind about that now," she said hastily. "I'm sorry I brought it up. It's really got nothing to do with it, except that I felt muddled about us, and I wanted to talk to Daddy. Only he wasn't sleeping, and he wasn't in our family unit. I went up to Admin and checked his office and he wasn't there either."

"So? Ann, what are you fussing about? He could have been in any one of a dozen places."

"But he wasn't! I've been looking for him ever since, and he isn't anywhere. He hasn't even been home, but I distinctly heard his secretary telling callers that he was home with a viral infection. No visitors allowed, she said, and she was to put all his calls through to the Administrative Assistant."

"Mary Macasey? Did you talk to her?"

"Well of course I did. And she had the same story. She's been told to handle all financial business until the Comptroller gets back."

"And he's not in your family unit?"

"*No.* I told you that."

"Wait a minute. The hospital! Did you think of the hospital?"

"Kep, you must think I'm a perfect idiot. Of course I did. He's not there. He never was. He's nowhere on the Base."

"Did this ever happen before?"

"Well, he's been away from home a great deal, especially in the last two years, but he's always let me know where he was and when he'd be back, always. This time it's different."

"Well, don't get so frantic. It's probably just a misunderstanding. If he's not on Base then he's somewhere else on Moon. There are plenty of places, for goodness sake . . . Copernicus, Alphonsus, Serenity, the Imbrium Terminal, Aristarchus . . ."

"Well, that's one place he couldn't be," she interrupted. "Not even the Governor could be in Aristarchus right now. Not with LEMCON feelings the way they are. But I've checked everywhere else on Moon, every single place. And nobody's seen him."

"Ann, let me get this straight. Dawn was sixteen watches ago. Are you really telling me that you haven't seen your father for sixteen watches and that nobody knows where he is?"

"Yes, Kep. That's what I'm saying. Why are you so slow?" She wrung her hands. "Something awful's happened to him, and nobody'll tell me. They're all covering up. Why? I've got to find out."

I thought hard. "Well, your mother must know where he is. Haven't you asked her?"

"Oh, Kep, really. Of course I asked her."

"And?"

"She just looked vague in that maddening way she has and said, 'If Admin says he's home with a virus, then that's where he is. Don't fuss, Ann.' Then she went back to her microscope. She's impossible. You can't talk to her."

I grinned. Dr Beth Sheppard was a micro-biologist and a Nobel prize-winner, and I knew exactly what Ann meant. But surely . . .

"If anything really awful happened to your Father they'd have had to tell her, wouldn't they? And even in the middle of an experiment . . . I mean, news like that would be bound to sink in, wouldn't it?"

"I really wonder," Ann said helplessly. "But what I think is that they're keeping it from her so as not to disturb her work."

"It? What sort of *it* do you think it is?"

"Whatever's happened to Daddy. Personally I think he's been kidnapped."

"Kidnapped? Really, Ann, this is Moon, not Earth. And by whom, for Pete's sake?"

"I don't know. LEMCON maybe. Don't laugh. They might, you know. They're really boiling at the UN decision."

"But what possible use would kidnapping your father be? After all, it was *my* father who negotiated the treaty. Surely if they were going to abduct someone, he would be the more logical choice. Anyway . . ."

I stopped abruptly, and started thinking hard. I was remembering my own experience in Aristarchus. It didn't seem reasonable that there should be *two* sets of thugs working for the LEMCON shareholders back on Earth. If Clint had been holding Dr Sheppard as hostage against a softer attitude towards the mines on the part of Moon colony, he should have been absolutely delighted when I fell into his hands, like an unexpected bonus. But he hadn't been a bit pleased. He couldn't wait to get me out of there, to the extent of trying to murder me. So he couldn't possibly be responsible for abducting Dr Sheppard. And if not Clint, then surely not LEMCON. But I couldn't explain any of my reasoning to Ann. I'd promised Father . . .

"No," I finished flatly. "I don't think it makes sense, Ann. Anyway, what about Father? Have you talked to him?"

"Certainly I have. I saw him for about two minutes. I told him Daddy wasn't home or at work, or anywhere on Moon that I could discover. He listened to me in that serious polite way of his, you know, Kep." She put the tips of her fingers together and looked at me over the top of them.

I laughed. It was so like Father. "Well, what did he say?"

"He said, and I quote: 'I strongly advise you to listen to your Mother, Ann, and leave things alone.' And then . . ." She hesitated.

"Then?"

"It was really most peculiar. He said: 'For your father's sake, Ann, and yours.' It was almost like a threat, but that doesn't make sense. He must have meant that something bad has happened, like kidnapping."

I shook my head helplessly. "Didn't you ask him?"

"I didn't get the chance. End of interview. I was brushed out of there like a speck of moon-dust. Do you ever get the feeling, Kep, that the adults don't really think we're people at all? A year ago I didn't think of questioning what Father was doing or where he was. But I'm an adult now, Kep. Nearly. And I want to know what's going on. But now I'm afraid to go on asking questions, in case your father meant it seriously, about my leaving things alone."

"Then why tell me? What can *I* do? I mean, you know I'd do anything for you I could, Ann. But what *can* I do? Maybe you'd be better just to take Father's advice and back off."

Ann shook her head. Then she leaned across the table and dropped her voice to a whisper, even though the cubicle was sound-proofed. "There's something more. Something awful. I . . . I went into Daddy's room and searched it."

"You did *what*?" I stared at her. Our sleeping cubicles were all that we had that was private, and nobody would ever go into another person's unit, much less touch his belongings. That Ann of all people, always so perfect and prim, should break this unwritten law, was unbelievable. Unless she was desperately frightened . . .

She blushed and her eyes dropped. "Kep, I had to. Do you see? I was frantic. Everyone was lying. I didn't know where to turn, or who to trust. I thought if I went through his things I might find a clue."

"That was a bit far-fetched, wasn't it?" I said, and then it suddenly struck me as comic that I should be scandalised by Ann's behaviour instead of the other way around. I grinned. "And of course you didn't find anything."

"But I *did*. That's the whole point. That's why I need your help, Kep. I can't do it alone."

"Do what?"

"Go after Daddy. I know where he's gone. Or been taken. Look, Kep." She fished in the breast pocket of her uniform and handed me a folded piece of paper.

I pressed it open on the table and stared at it. It was a sketch map of part of the western hemisphere of Moon. It was bounded, top and bottom, by the thirtieth degree north latitude and the equator, and on the sides by the longitudes of twenty degrees west and a hundred and ten west. Near the right margin was the triangle of the populated craters of Copernicus, Aristarchus and Kepler, the heart of Moon colony. On this map they were lightly indicated. The detailed work lay to the west, beyond that part of Moon inhabited either by colonists or by LEMCON.

"So – a Moon map." I stared at Ann.

"Kep, look at the trail that's marked. See where it's leading. Into

Earthdark!"

I looked again, almost unbelievingly.

From Kepler Base a dotted line ran west-north-west across the Ocean of Storms, past Marius crater to the spot where one of the early Russian probes had landed, way back in the 1960's. From there the dotted line moved westward, taking the easiest way between the ancient, almost obliterated walls of Eddington and Struve, past Balboa to Moseley, right on the ninetieth degree of longitude, the edge of Moon's visible disc. But the map did not stop there. It, and the dotted line marked on it, continued west around in to what Earth people still call "the dark side of the Moon".

How strangely self-centred Earth people are, I thought, as I stared at the map. To them the face of the Moon that *they* saw was light, and the face that was turned away from Earth was called dark. In reality, of course, the sun shone equally all round Moon, for two weeks out of every four. Only once you passed the ninetieth degree of longitude the Earth, sinking lower behind the opposite horizon, finally ceased to occupy a visible place in Moon's sky. It was as Earthdark, not Moondark, that the colonists described the far side of Moon.

"Well?" Ann's voice broke in on my thoughts.

"Well, what?" I blinked.

"The map. I think that's where Daddy's been taken."

"Ann, it's impossible. Nobody lives in Earthdark, you know that. By the time you get as far west as Moseley Earth is so low in the sky that communications are almost impossible."

"I don't care. Just look at the map. That dotted line is a trail, isn't it? It starts at the 'X' in Kepler Crater, and it finishes right in that crater there, in Earthdark, the crater marked 'X'." She stabbed at it with her finger.

"This map doesn't have to mean a thing, you know. It might just as well be a joke, a doodle, anything."

"Hidden in Daddy's sleep cubicle?"

"*Hidden*? Aren't you exaggerating just a bit, Ann? Surely you mean left, discarded, whatever?"

She shook her head. "I mean hidden. I was looking in his drawer

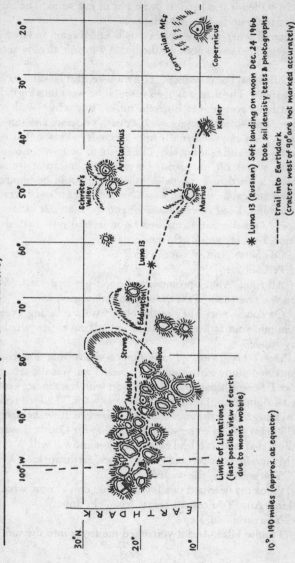

HUNTLEY SHEPPARD'S MAP (with some additions)

Copernicus

Carpathian Mts

Kepler

Aristarchus

Schröter's Valley

Marius

Luna 13

Eddington

Struve

Moseley

Balboa

EARTHDARK

Limit of Librations
(last possible view of earth
due to moon's wobble)

10° = 190 miles (approx. at equator)

✳ Luna 13 (Russian) Soft landing on moon Dec. 24 1966
  took soil density tests & photographs

------ trail into Earthdark
  (craters west of 90° are not marked accurately)

20°   30°   40°   50°   60°   70°   80°   90°   100°W

30°N

20°

10°

and I pulled it too hard. It came out in my hand. The map was taped to the underside of the drawer."

I stared at her, and then picked up the map again and looked at it closely. There was nothing there that I hadn't already seen. But still . . .

"All right. I'm convinced it isn't a joke. But he can't have been kidnapped. The map was in *his* room. If he went into Earthdark he must have gone under his own steam. But why? With whom? There's no colony there. LEMCON doesn't operate any mines over there. They can't. After all, Ann, it stands to reason that with no atmosphere and nothing else, like Earth, to bounce radio and television waves off, there can be no communication for anyone farther apart than a couple of miles. Life would be impossible."

She shrugged. "I know, Kep. I've been over it and over it in my own mind. But Father *is* missing, and the map *was* hidden in his room. And the trail is marked right around into Earthdark. So please, Kep, say you'll help me."

"Of course, Ann. What can I do?"

"Promise me."

"All right, Ann, I promise. Just don't get hysterical. What do you want me to do? Take the map to Father and . . ."

"Of course not! They're the ones who are hiding everything from me, your father and Admin . . . talking to *him* wouldn't do any good."

"Don't cry, Ann." I was horror-struck that my cool self-contained moon girl should fall apart. That was the second time since I'd come home that I'd seen Ann with tears in her eyes. "It'll be all right, Ann. I'll do whatever you want," I added recklessly. Anything to stop the tears that ran unchecked down her face.

"I want you to come with me looking for Daddy. I want us to follow that map. It'll lead us to him, I just know it will."

My mouth fell open and I stared at her, earthstruck.

"You *promised*," she wailed.

I shook my head and swallowed. "You don't know what you're asking, Ann. You're mad, crazy. It can't be done."

"You promised, Kep."

"I know I did. And if you asked me to fly into the sun, would

66

you expect me to go along with it? It's impossible for us to go alone into Earthdark. Do you even realise how far it is?"

"Twelve hundred miles." She blew her nose and sniffed.

"One way. It's another twelve hundred back, you know. That's if you planned on coming back! It's night time now, so we couldn't use a brolly, and the stripways certainly don't run through into Earthdark, so how do you expect to get there? We couldn't take a crawler. They just don't have the range."

"We don't have to take a crawler. There's another way."

"Well, I'd certainly like to hear what it is," I said sarcastically. As if I didn't know all there was to know about Moon vehicles.

"I'll tell you about it later. Only take my word for it, Kep. There *is* another way."

"All right. What about navigating, then? Do you realise what it would be like?"

"You got safely up the terminator and back. And you were alone. That's what gave me the idea."

I groaned. "Look, Ann, that trip was dumb. I was lucky, that's all. And I had full navigational aids to fall back on — the Sun, Earth, radio beacons, the lot. Over into Earthdark there'd be nothing but the stars and the inertial navigation system. One miscalculation, just two miles off the correct course, and you could be lost for ever. There aren't even any landmarks over there, and I'm not a trained pilot or navigator."

"I could navigate, Kep. I know I could. I'm good, really. Trust me."

"Trust you!" I tried to run my fingers through my hair, forgetting it had been cut short in a moon crop now. "Oh, Ann, in the mood you're in I wouldn't trust you to navigate across a teacup. Look, I've got to go. I can't miss another lab, not while I'm still under penalty. Let me take the map. I'll talk to Father and make him listen. Don't worry. It'll all work out."

I snatched up the map and my books and left her sitting in the study cubicle while I ran for the elevator. For the rest of my work day I found it was hard to concentrate. The picture of Ann, sitting forlorn and white-faced where I'd left her, kept getting in the way.

Chapter Seven

SINCE RETURNING to Moon I'd really been disenchanted with Ann. It wasn't just that I didn't love her. I guess I'd never feel about her quite the way I felt about Hilary. I know we were due to be married in three years, but that had been a decision of the colony psychologists, not of either Ann's or mine.

To them it had seemed that we were compatible. Love had nothing much to do with it. Courting, rivalries, playing the field, all the premarital games of kids on Earth, had always been forbidden on Moon. In a tiny closed society like ours it would have been about as safe as introducing a box of dynamite into an ore smelter.

At age fourteen we were paired by the psychologists, and that was that. I was resigned to not really *loving* Ann, but since I'd come back to Moon I had found that I didn't even *like* her very much. She was just too smooth, too cool, too darn perfect.

Now all of a sudden I was seeing a different Ann, not the same girl at all. I was seeing her in tears, off balance, jittery. I was seeing her break rules, her precious unbreakable moon rules. And above all I was seeing her needing me. It made me feel very protective, a most unaccustomed emotion — around Ann.

As soon as I was finished with classes I went up to Father's office. He was working late as usual, and the outer office was deserted. Tommy was still at her desk, though, and Father's door was shut.

"I've got to see him," I said without preamble.

"I'm sorry, Kep. He's in conference."

"I'll wait."

"But you can't do that! I mean, I don't know how long he's going to be. It could be hours. Why don't you go up and have

68

your dinner and then come back?"

"I might miss him that way. And this is very important." I sat down directly outside Father's door and crossed my legs.

Tommy got up from her desk and hovered helplessly. "Kep, please get up and go away. You really shouldn't be here. Your father's going to be so mad. And you'll get me into trouble," she added.

"I'm sorry about that, Tommy, but I'm going to stay anyway. Why don't *you* go and get your dinner? No point in both of us going hungry. I'll hold the fort until you get back, I promise."

"I can't persuade you to go away?"

"I'm not budging, Tommy."

"Well . . ." She stood uncertainly over me. I was about a foot taller and fifty Earth-pounds heavier. "Well, I suppose I might as well go and get something to eat. I won't be long. Back in twenty minutes. You'll tell him if . . ."

"Don't fuss, Tommy. I'll tell him I sent you off screaming and kicking, and that you didn't abandon your post willingly."

She left. It had been quite easy after all. I sprawled in my chair and chortled inside. I thought of all the times I'd wanted to talk to Father and let myself be put off by secretaries and protocol and all the grown-up barrage of words that they put up around themselves. And all I had had to do was to be firm.

I waited for ten minutes. Fifteen. Eighteen. I pricked up my ears. A chair scraped across the vinyl floor and there were voices close to the door. ". . . if you don't, Dr Sheppard'll be for it, I warn you!" I jumped to my feet but I hadn't time to get out of the way of the door before the man was out. He was so fast and so light on his feet that he caught me off balance.

"Watch it, son." He held my forearms and moved me to one side. For a second our glances met. His hands tightened, though I'll swear his face never changed, not by a flicker. But the grip of his hands was enough. I stared at him intently.

It was a very unmemorable face, bland and blond and undistinguished, except for two extraordinary features. One of his eyes was blue and the other a light hazel brown. It was an oddity that I'd never come across before. Or had I? Memory pricked at my mind like a tiresome thorn. And like an arrow drawing attention to the freakishness of his eyes, a puckered scar ran white from the corner of the cheek bone to the left eye, the blue one.

In another second he was gone, moving as swiftly and competently as an athlete. The outer office was empty and I was left facing Father in the doorway to his office. I wasn't sure if he was more angry than surprised, or the other way around.

"It's my fault, not Tommy's," I said hastily, remembering my bargain. "She really did try to throw me out, but I wouldn't let her."

"I see. I'm glad she's not to blame. What is it, Kepler? I presume it must be important, but I really have very little time."

"Yes, sir." My hand went to my pocket, touching Dr Sheppard's map. Where *had* I seen that man before? It couldn't be important compared with Dr Sheppard's disappearance, and yet . . . "Father, who *was* that? He doesn't belong on Kepler, and yet I'm sure I've seen him before."

"You may have. He's been up on Moon for discussion with me for eighteen days. He came up on the last midnight ferry."

"Who is he?"

"My liaison with the UN." Father spoke smoothly, and there was no reason in the world for me to disbelieve him. He'd never lied to me before. And yet . . .

The UN . . . The moritorium . . . LEMCON . . . Aristarchus . . . flashed through my mind, and then I remembered exactly where and when I'd seen Scarface, the so-called UN liaison officer.

He had been among the crowd of miners coming off shift just as Clint and Blue were hustling me off the LEMCON Base in Aristarchus. It was he who had jostled my arm then. And he had recognised me just now. I was sure of that. . . .

"Kep, are you all right? You're as white as a sheet. Sit down, son."

I swallowed and got a grip on myself. "I'm fine, Father. Guess I shouldn't have skipped dinner, that's all. I'll go on up now, before the cafeteria closes. UN liaison, you said? I suppose he was one of the people you got to know when we were down on Earth? And he's been in Kepler since last midnight, eh?"

"Yes, that's right. We're working together. Kep, what on Moon is the matter with you?"

"Nothing, I'm fine, really."

"You said you wanted to see me about something important. Tell me about it. I can make the time. Don't worry."

"No, thanks. It's all right. I . . . I've changed my mind. I'm sorry I barged in like that. I'll talk to you another time. Right now I'd better go for dinner." Still burbling I blundered through the outer door, smack into Tommy hurrying back to her post.

As the elevator door slid shut between us I had the clearest picture of her standing staring after me, and beyond her, outside the inner office, my father.

I didn't go up to the cafeteria. Instead I punched "3" and went down to Dormitory "A". I didn't let myself begin to think until the door of my private sleep cubicle was shut safely behind me.

Father had lied to me. To *me*. In my whole life I never remembered Father as being anything less than perfectly open and straightforward. And now he had lied to me. To protect a LEMCON man.

I stood with my back against the door and struggled to keep calm and open-minded. By my bed the fragile tower of balsa wood stood, its many-coloured tissue shapes trembling in the faint breeze from the air duct. It looked perfectly ridiculous and childish. I found I was sobbing, great dry sobs that tore at my chest, and I beat at the tower with my fists, tearing the tissue and shredding the balsa wood laths into splinters. Then I threw myself face down on my bed.

After a long while I began to think again. Why had Father lied? Why should he have gone to the trouble of telling me that Scarface had been with him on Kepler, when I knew perfectly well that he'd been working in Aristarchus? Though Father didn't know that I'd seen him, or did he? I rolled over and stared at the ceiling.

I was sure that I'd never mentioned the miners I'd met in the passage to Father, because they had really nothing to do with the story. So as far as Father was concerned Scarface's cover story was perfectly air-tight.

What was the connection between the neatly uniformed liaison officer in Father's office and the sweaty unshaved miner who'd jostled me in the air-lock passage? *Why* was Father lying for a LEMCON man? And what was a LEMCON man doing in Kepler? And in Father's private office? Come to that, why had Tommy lied to me earlier and told me that Father was in Aristarchus himself? Father couldn't have got into Aristarchus, not unless he was working for LEMCON instead of Moon. No, that last was impossible. Father couldn't be a traitor, not possibly. Not Father. Not unless, somehow, he was in LEMCON's power. What were those words I'd heard, muffled by Father's office door? . . . "If you don't Dr Sheppard'll be for it. I warn you!"

A thought flashed through my mind that sent the blood from my face. I sat up and swung my legs to the floor. Just suppose that LEMCON *had* abducted Dr Sheppard. They could be forcing Father to do what they wanted by threatening to kill Ann's father.

The more I thought about it, the more air-tight it seemed to be. Ann was right all along and I was wrong. Someone in LEMCON, someone not in with Clint, had kidnapped Dr Sheppard. And that was why Father was so peculiar, never to be found, tired and distracted, lying about where he had been, lying about Dr Sheppard, lying about Scarface.

Scarface. *He* had to be here on Kepler Base to keep an eye on Father, to make sure he didn't talk, and to make sure he lived up to his side of whatever infamous bargain he had had to strike with them.

I must talk to Ann. Right now. I walked out, leaving the splinters of balsa wood and shreds of tissue where they'd fallen.

'B' watch was working, and she wasn't in a lab where I might have sneaked in and got hold of her, but in one of the big lecture halls. I had to wait in the hall, eaten up with impatience, for two solid hours, until the doors finally opened and the students came pouring out.

She saw me right away, and hurried over, dodging through the crowd. She stood in front of me with her arms full of books and looked up at me without saying anything for a long moment.

Then, "Oh, Kep, you'll do it? You'll come?"

I nodded.

"Oh, Kep, thank you. I'm so grateful. What made you change your mind?"

"I don't want to talk about it. I'll drive you into Earthdark, but I don't want you going on about it."

"All right, Kep." She put a hand on my arm. "All right."

"The first thing we've got to do is to plan this thing properly. Let's go back to the library."

Safe in the sound-proof cubicle of a study room we sat on either side of the little table and worked out the details of our odyssey into Earthdark.

"The vehicle's the vital thing, Ann. Honestly, we couldn't make it in a crawler. Did you really mean it when you said there was something else?"

She nodded. "The engineers have developed a new car, a sort of rugged camper, I guess you could call it. It's built a bit like a crawler, but wider and much longer, with a bunk and table and cooking and toilet facilities."

"How does it run?" I was sceptical. It sounded punishingly heavy, even on Moon.

"Much the same as a crawler, I believe. There are battery motors on the wheels for slow speeds and manoeuvring, and standard jets for cruising. The fuel tanks seemed very large, at least three thousand mile capacity, I'd guess, and the batteries are a new design."

I whistled. "It sounds fantastic. But how come you know so much about it and I've never even heard a whisper?"

"But you have, Kep. Or something very like it. You saw the plans yourself when you did your stint in drafting before you went down to Earth, oh, it must be almost a year ago."

"Those." My heart sank. "Oh, Ann, that was just an experimental design. There wasn't even a prototype."

She grinned suddenly, engagingly. "Well, there is now. Better. There are three of them. Operational models. I've seen them myself."

"Where?"

"They're hidden in one of those old blow-out caves under the rim of the crater, up in the north-west quadrant."

"Hidden? Really? Why? Who built them? Whose are they?

73

And how in Moon did you ever find them?"

"I can't even begin to answer your first questions, or half a dozen more I've been asking myself since I saw them. But as to how I found them, well, the map led me there."

"It did?" I took the map out of my pocket and smoothed it out on the table. "I don't get it."

"Well, I was getting desperate about Daddy and I couldn't get any answers from anyone. I kept coming back to the map. It was the only thing I had that connected with Daddy, and from the way it had been hidden I knew it was the key to the whole thing. But the more I looked at it, the more it puzzled me. It's only a rough sketch, but the trail has been marked so carefully, all the way from that cross in Kepler over to Marius, and from Marius up to Luna 13, and then west over into Earthdark, to that other cross in the crater over there."

"Yes, I see. But . . ."

"And the paper. It's such an awkward shape. A long skinny strip."

"Well, it had to be, to fit the whole trail on and keep a true scale," I pointed out. "I mean, that's the way it is..It's got to cover seventy degrees east and west, and only twenty north and south. Of course it's wide and skinny. But what do the proportions matter? I mean, this isn't an art appreciation course, is it?"

"Funny! Look, Kep. Why would anybody that knew Moon at all bother to mark the trail from Kepler to Luna 13? Kepler's the heart of the colony and Luna 13 is a famous landmark. It's marked on every map that ever was. So why couldn't whoever made this sketch originally have started at Luna 13 and marked only the unknown part of the trail, from there over into Earthdark?"

"I see what you mean. And then it would have fitted on a standard piece of paper. He wouldn't have had to cut a sheet of drafting paper to fit. So what you're saying, Ann, is that the part of the map between Kepler and Luna 13 is *specially* important, so it had to be included in the map."

She nodded. "Can you guess now?"

"No. But I know you can't wait to tell me."

"It's the cross in Kepler. I thought, maybe it does more than just mark the beginning of the trail. Maybe the cross itself means something. So I took out a jet-pack and I went over to the north-west corner of the rim, about where the two arms of the cross intersect, and I found it. A blow-out cave with three campers, brand new, parked in it."

I stared at her as if I were seeing her for the first time. She was full of surprises. She'd always had a brain, but I wouldn't have called her imaginative. "Ann, you're marvellous. I wouldn't have worked that out in a million years."

She went pink. "Oh, well. Anyway, maybe they've all gone by now. It was two watches ago that I saw them. We'll have to check again."

I sagged. "And it's night time, when every vehicle that can be scrounged from anywhere is out. Bother!"

"I don't think just anyone will have taken them." She spoke slowly. "I think they are there for a special reason, though I don't know what. But they were really hidden."

"*You* found them."

"That was partly luck. I mean, I was looking for something, only I didn't know what. You can't even see the cave at night, probably only at dawn when there's a good shadow. But you see I have this compass . . ."

"Compass!"

"Don't laugh. A favourite cousin gave it to me when I came up to Moon. He didn't know that compasses were useless on Moon, that there just isn't a steady magnetic field up here. Well, I didn't know it then either. After all, we were both only kids. Anyway I was bitterly disappointed when we got up here and I found I couldn't use it. So Daddy had it made into a lucky charm. And I always carry it, every time I go out."

"I never noticed it, Ann."

"There's a lot of things you haven't noticed about me, Kep. I wear it clipped to my moon suit belt, always. So, anyway, I was drifting along under the crater wall when I suddenly noticed my old compass give a kick."

"Didn't you think it was just a mass concentration? After all, the *maria* are loaded with magnetic areas like that."

75

"At first I did. But it wasn't out under the *mare*, where you'd expect a mascon to be. It was close by. My compass would swither one way, and a few yards further on it would swither back. So I looked closely and found the cave."

"And a ton or so of metal for the compass to have reacted to?" She nodded.

"You're some girl, Ann. All right, let's say we can get a camper. Then we're going to need food concentrate for two or four days, two days out and two back."

"More. We'll have Daddy on the way back."

I looked across the table at her. Her dark eyes told me nothing. Did she really believe that we'd find him, or was she whistling in the dark? But I nodded. "Fair enough. Let's say food, water and oxygen for three people for four days, plus a couple of days leeway for accidents. I wonder how on Moon we'll manage to carry all that out of the Base without being seen."

"The oxygen cylinders and the water-tanks were full when I looked at the campers. They seemed to be completely fitted up and ready to go."

"We must check that before we go, but okay. Now, how are you going to go about stealing the food?"

Ann blenched at the word "steal", but I'd said it deliberately. I didn't want her getting cold feet half way through the operation. Even for a kid to sneak an extra biscuit was considered an antisocial act on Moon. To exceed your designated caloric allotment was not only unhealthy, but meant that you would be depriving a fellow-colonist. And that for a biscuit. To take enough food for three people for six days . . .

"Oh, Kep. Do I have to?"

"You know I'm still on penalty, Ann. I mustn't be caught hanging around the kitchens. But if you can't do it, we can call the whole thing off."

She swallowed. "I . . . I'll do it during 'A' watch's dinner hour. The kitchen staff will all be at the servers. The store-rooms should be completely empty."

"How long'll that be?"

She glanced at her watch. "It's 2230 hours now. Less than two

76

hours to wait. What'll I do with the stuff?"

I thought for a minute. "Take it up to low-temperature engineering. There'll be nobody up there, they'll all be out on the surface. I'll meet you there."

"All right. And, Kep – thank you."

"It's for myself too, Ann." I didn't tell her it was really for Father, that I'd do anything, even go on a lost-cause hunt over into Earthdark, if it might get Father out of the hands of Scarface and LEMCON. "Look, if the campers aren't as fully operational as you thought, we'll have to come back for water and oxygen. And fuel . . . what about fuel! Remember I'm still grounded. I mustn't let anyone see me outside, or anywhere else I'm not supposed to be, for that matter."

"Oh, Kep, will your father *kill* you?"

"Not if it all comes out right."

"And if it doesn't. Suppose . . ."

"Then to tell you the truth I won't really care. But it'll work out. Now you'd better head off and do whatever you're supposed to be doing right now, and so must I. We don't want people asking awkward questions."

We met as we had planned, at 0030 hours on the fourth day of the lunar night. The watches had just changed. My watch was down in "A" dormitory sleeping. Nobody would look for me for eight clear hours. Ann's watch was on recreation and study, followed by sleep, so she should be clear for sixteen hours. It couldn't have worked out better.

The dome was deserted as we sneaked cautiously out of the elevator, each carrying a big box of food concentrates. We parted outside the change rooms and I got my gear out of its locker in the men's change room. I felt better in the anonymity of a moon suit. One person in silver coveralls and a white helmet with gold-tinted visor looked much like another, and in the dark of night, with everybody on Moon's surface busy about his own business, there was little reason for anyone to challenge me, or get close enough to read my shoulder patches or name tag.

Ann and I emerged together and helped each other into jetpacks. Then we picked up the food boxes and locked through to

77

Moon surface.

Ann adjusted her pack and drifted off to the left, a silver moth in the dark, with me close behind her. For short-range travel there's nothing like jetting. There's no noise, of course, just a gentle tugging of the harness beneath your arms. There's no wind stream and gravity is little more than a sense of right-way-upness, as you drift along, a foot or so off the ground, with nothing between you and the endless blackness, dense with stars, but the thin shell of a space visor. Below your feet the ground is close enough to see every speck and pock mark, every glisten of glass, the million delicate pastel shades of moon-dust stained by the proximate minerals.

We jetted across the ten mile span from Kepler Base to the crater rim in fifteen minutes, and it took Ann only another five to relocate the hidden ` garage" with her lucky-charm compass.

We flashed our lights through the pitch black interior. It was a perfect hiding place, this old blow-out cave.

When the colonists first arrived on Moon they had had to build temporary shelters, atmospherically safe and temperature controlled, while they were getting on with the job of excavating Moon and building the permanent underground homes and laboratories. The quickest, safest and cheapest way was to locate an area in a crater wall where the rock was particularly weak and porous. A single charge of explosive would usually be enough to punch a hole in it the size of a squash court. This was completely lined with a spray plastic, which dried rock-hard, and made an insulating impervious barrier to the cold and vacuum of Moon. Once it was fitted with a pre-fabricated air-lock, hauled up in one piece from Earth, it became a safe, though crowded, temporary home. Once the underground facilities were completed these temporary shelters were dismantled, the air-locks removed and they were abandoned.

The hidden garage was one of these. And there was ample room in it for the three brand new "campers" it contained. Not to mention the oxygen cylinders, the spare batteries and the fuel drums piled along the back wall.

I put my helmet against Ann's so that we could talk. It was too dark in there to lip-read. "Who do you suppose put these in here?

Who would know about it? I never did, and I've been here all my life."

"Only the people that were actually here when Kepler was being built, I suppose." Her voice sounded hollow, metallic, like a robot, from inside her helmet. Not like Ann at all.

She and her father and mother had only been on Moon for five years. There were not that many charter members of Moon colony still on Kepler. A dozen, perhaps, no more, who would know about the cave. My father was one of them.

Chapter Eight

ANN WAS IN A FEVER of impatience to be off, but I refused to let myself be hurried. We were perfectly safe from observation inside the cave. On a moon without atmosphere there was no such thing as a beam of light. Our flashlights showed only small circles of gold in the darkness, and threw ellipses of light only on to the solid objects at which we pointed them. The chance of anybody else being in a direct line-of-sight position with the lens of one of our flashlights was remote enough not to be considered.

I chose the camper parked closest to the exit, the one that would be the easiest to get out of the cave, and I explored it thoroughly, inside and out. The vehicle *had* been used. There was a particle or two of moon-dust clinging to the silicone grease that lubricated its moving parts, and one of the teflon-coated valves bore a few minute scratch marks. But it was to all intents and purposes brand-new. And beautiful. It was, as Ann had said, a development of the all-purpose little crawler, but roomier, more powerful, and very ruggedly constructed. When had it been made, I wondered, as I looked it over? When? And where? And above all, *why* should it have been made in secret and hidden in this secret cave?

We took the packages of food concentrate inside and stowed them away, and checked out the fuel, water, oxygen and the lithium oxides that were used in the scrubbers to get rid of the carbon dioxide that we breathed out. Everything was in order. The water had that lifeless taste of stored water, but it was perfectly drinkable. In fact it didn't even taste re-cycled . . . curious.

I dogged the air-lock shut, checked the integrity of the seals, and finally removed my gauntlets and pushed up the visor of my helmet. Ann did the same, and we grinned at each other, half scared, half triumphant. So far, so good.

"Strap yourself in," I suggested. "I'm going to try and get out of the cave and over the crater wall without lights. We don't want to call attention to ourselves unnecessarily."

Ann did as I said without comment. Only her eyes looked very big and dark.

"It'll be easy." I was encouraging myself as much as her. "Earth is past her first quarter. There'll be plenty of light." But I put out the flashlights and sat in the dark until my eyes were able to tell the difference between the blackness of the cave wall and the less dense black of the crater floor outside.

I turned on the battery power and heard the engines hum sweetly into life. A deep breath. Both hands on the controls. We moved slowly forwards out of the secret cave, not even nudging the other two campers as we slid past them. I had to fire the jets to get us up the steep incline of the inner wall of Kepler, but there were several dozen crawlers working in Kepler and outside on the *mare*, and the twin glow from one more vehicle would probably never be noticed.

Up on top I glanced over my shoulder at the pin-points of light around the entrances to Kepler Base. It looked like a broken nest of scurrying fire-ants down there. On every side the *mare* stretched, featureless to the horizon, while the stars shone thick above, with Earth a huge silver-blue half disc, its night-side dusky red against the blackness of space.

I wondered how long it would be before we saw Kepler Base again. If we ever would see it again. I took a deep steadying breath, settled myself in the driver's seat and cinched my harness tight.

We headed west-north-west across the Ocean of Storms, keeping Earth at our backs. I never did switch on the headlights. Our eyes were becoming adjusted, and starlight and earthshine between them gave a faint even illumination that coloured the dusty surface dark brown. There was not enough depth of shadow to show up small faults and debris, but the shocks of the camper were sturdily designed and made, and it rode twice as well as a crawler.

In under two hours the relatively smooth surface began to be broken by large rilles and wrinkle ridges. I had to steer clear of them, but their presence there was cheering.

"Your navigation is right on the button, Ann. Marius Crater should be coming up on our left any moment now."

"There it is, Kep." She leaned over my shoulder to point. "At least I suppose it *is* Marius."

I laughed. From the surface of the *mare*, with a horizon limited to a mile and a half, one crater tended to look very much like another, just a rise in the surface and a faint change in colour from the dark three billion year old basalt of the *mare* to the paler crust material thrown up and out in the impact that formed the original crater. We could see some of this material now, lumps of faintly paler breccia scattered on the dark dust of the *mare*.

"There's nothing else but Marius on this heading, Ann, so you've nothing to worry about. Your navigation is dead on. But I've been thinking. When we get over to Earthdark we'll only have the stars and the inertial navigator to go by. It'll be very tricky and you'll have some fussy maths. Why don't you see if you can get us to Luna 13 from here without relying on the radio beacons or Earth position? If you find you can't do it, we'd better know now, before it's too late."

Ann nodded and pulled out the small lap desk in front of her. Then she reached over and switched off the radio beacon without another word. Her hand was firm and I glanced across at her with admiration. That act took quite a lot of faith. It was like setting out on a cross-country walk blindfold.

"No cheating now," I teased her. "You mustn't peep back at Earth."

She just smiled and set to work, and in five minutes handed me a course correction. Now that we were actually doing something that might help her father she was her calm self again, and I'd have trusted her maths to pin-point us anywhere in the Galaxy.

We jetted on in silence across the silent *mare*. The Ocean of Storms. It was a funny name for the ancients to have given it, these half million square miles of dusty basaltic plain spattered with impact craters, untouched by wind and water since the beginnings of time.

Beyond Marius the rilles and wrinkle ridges starfished out, and I wound my way between them until we were in the clear again, hoping that Ann and the inertial navigator were keeping track of my movements.

Another course correction, a small one. One hour had passed. Then two. Finding Luna 13 on the wide surface of the *mare* was a bit like homing in on a buoy in mid-Atlantic.

"Five minutes, Kep." Ann broke the silence. I nodded and stared ahead.

"Two minutes."

"We'd better have a light." I switched on the searchlight mounted outside the driving compartment of the camper, and played it to and fro, so that a long ellipse of light ran across the dark surface of the *mare* nearly a quarter of a mile ahead of us.

"One minute."

I slowed down. Whatever happened we mustn't miss the moon probe. From it we had to set our new course westerly, and then drive by dead-reckoning into Earthdark.

I stared ahead. Was that a flash? I blinked and swept the searchlight across from left to right. There it was, Luna 13, right on the button. Ahead of us, less than fifty feet to our right. I switched off our jets and coasted in on the battery motors. "Fantastic navigation, Ann. Congratulations."

She smiled her small neat smile, but didn't answer me. As I cut the searchlight and the motors she fastened her clipboard and stylo to their place on the navigator's table.

I left the auxiliary battery to run the heater and the interior lights. We blinked and stretched. After nearly four hours without moving, it was wonderful to be able to get up and stroll around. With the lights on, the camper was like a cheerful little home, warm and secure. The lights pushed the lonely darkness of the *mare* away from the windows, and our world shrank from a universe to forty square feet.

We ate standing up, just a protein biscuit and our allotment of water, but I still felt I needed to get the fidgets out of my legs.

"Come on. Let's go out and take a look at it close up," I persuaded Ann. I knew she wanted to waste not a single minute, but I knew too I couldn't drive safely if I had cramps in my legs. We fastened down our visors and put on our gauntlets, checked each other's breathing pack and then went through the two-man lock to Moon surface.

Luna 13 sat in the dust exactly where it had landed at Christmas time, thirty-nine years before. We walked around it, our feet scuffing the foot-prints of other colonists who had come out to this deserted sector of the Ocean of Storms to see the ancient Russian moon probe.

I tried to imagine what it must have been like back then, before men had colonised Moon. It had been Russia versus the United States back in those days, competing with each other in their extravagant race for Moon. Now all that was over. Moon's colonists came from every country on Earth, and its charter was under the jurisdiction of the United Nations. Even LEMCON, I remembered, was a member of an international cartel.

We shot Earth position against the stars, and checked the inertial navigator against our readings and against the radio beacon position. Everything tallied. Everything was working perfectly and now we both felt confident that Ann's maths would be more than good enough to navigate us safely into Earthdark and back again.

Ann was still silent and withdrawn. Her tension worried me. I made her play tag with me before we went back inside. We kept within sight of the camper all the time of course, loping out a mile and then back again. She was chasing me when I suddenly noticed something that made me stop dead in my tracks. She bumped into me and we both fell over. Our fall was soft enough under moon-grav, and we lay in a tangle of boots and helmets and breathing packs and laughed till we were out of breath.

It was good to be laughing again. Crazy, but good. She leant against me so that our helmets touched. "Oh, Kep, that's better. I've been feeling so dreadful. Stealing the food, and the camper. Doing all those awful things. Kep, am I right?"

"Sure you are." I helped her disentangle, and we got to our feet. "Don't worry so, Ann."

"What were you doing stopping like that?" She still held on to my arm.

I pointed to ground just ahead of us. As clearly marked as if they had been made five minutes ago, printed into the talc-fine moon-dust, were the tracks of another vehicle.

There had been plenty of track marks and footprints around Luna 13. It marked unofficially the position of "farthest west". But these tracks did not double back with the rest, south-east to Kepler and Copernicus, or east to the Carpathians or the Apennines. Straight as a ruler, lonely as a comet, they streaked due west into the unknown.

When Ann saw them the grip of her hand on my arm tightened until I could feel her gloved fingers biting right through my vac-suit. I unhitched her gently. "Wait here," I told her. "I'll bring the camper over, and we'll follow the trail. It'll make the navigating easier."

She nodded and I loped off at a slow steady moon run back to where we had parked the camper close by Luna 13. When I'd climbed aboard I could just see her from the driving cab, a tiny sur-realistic figure, silver against the brown of the Earth-lit *mare*. I drove the camper slowly towards her until I could see clearly the westward-leading tracks.

When she climbed aboard through the air-lock she was jittery with excitement. "Kep, it must be Daddy. I was right. The map was right."

"Hey, steady. You know they could have been made any time since Man has been on Moon. They'd still look as fresh."

Her face fell. "You're right. I suppose . . . they could have been made by someone else. On the other hand," she brightened. "It just as well could be Daddy."

"True enough. And as long as they stay on our heading we'll follow them. But keep your eye on the navigation anyway, won't you?"

Secretly I was beginning to think that it was odds on that we'd find a stalled vehicle at the track's end, fifty, maybe a hundred miles ahead. And I wondered how I would cope with Ann if we *did* find it, and the pilot's body was her father. Alone in the waste. No heat. No oxygen. Out west where we were heading a stalled camper would be beyond the help of any radio'd S.O.S. West into

Earthdark we'd really be alone.

If Ann had had her way I'd have driven clean on for twenty-four hours, but I'd missed one sleep period already, and my eyes were starting to play tricks on me. Mile after mile of desertlike *mare*, as brown as chocolate, unfolded ahead of us. Each mile looked like the mile before. There was nothing to see except the ruler-straight track ahead of us. I kept having the strange feeling that we were really standing still, and again and again I found myself checking the speedometer.

Finally I pulled up short. "What is it?" Ann's voice was sharp.

"I can't go on, Ann. We've got to have a decent meal and a few hours sleep."

"But . . ."

"Look, we've come better than half way. If I drive over a crater rim or hang us up on a rille or in a dust boil it won't get us there any quicker, will it? And it's too far to walk home. Come on, Ann. Let's break out the rations. I'm ready to drop."

We ate in the comfort of the sleeping compartment, sitting side by side on the bunk. The food was emergency stuff, synthetic protein and carbohydrate mix, spooned out of a carton and washed down with instant soup, made with the four ounces of our water ration. It was tasteless food and a bit gluey, but splendidly filling. We didn't talk after we'd eaten. Just switched off the light and went to sleep.

When I awoke I couldn't remember where I was, until I stretched and hit my feet against the driving cab partition. Ann was still sleeping, curled up like a cat.

I looked at my watch, and jumped up. "Ann, wake up." I shook her gently. "We've been asleep ten whole hours."

She blinked awake. "Shall I make breakfast?"

"No. We'd better start out. Time enough to eat when we're tired and have to rest."

With Ann constantly checking the navigation we drove westward. We crossed the remains of the enormous arena of Eddington crater, its floor flooded smooth with the basalt that had welled up through Moon's crust after the cataclysm that had formed the Ocean of Storms. We made good time there.

Fifty miles further on it was another story. "Oh, Kep, can't you go any faster?"

"Ann, if we got hung up somewhere there'd be no one to help us. I can't take risks. It's getting rougher every minute. We must be going through the remains of Struve. And it's not going to get any better. Just look at the map!"

Past Struve we were on the shore-line of the Ocean of Storms, the *mare* on which I had spent my whole life. Farthest west. It was an excitingly scary thought. From now on we would be threading our way between craters, most of them huge. I was out of my depth and a little afraid. I cut our speed to fifty miles an hour. Then to thirty.

"We'll never get there, Kep," Ann fretted, leaning over my shoulder. "Look, you're down to twenty-five!"

"Ann, stop fussing. I'm doing my best. Look, you'd better check our navigation again. In less than two hundred miles we'll be out of sight of Earth."

"I'm sorry." She went back to the navigator's table. "It's just . . . you know . . . worrying about Daddy."

I drove west in silence. Behind us the blue-white marble that was Earth dropped slowly towards the eastern horizon.

"It's gone," Ann said suddenly. "No more radio link." That was all it meant to her.

To me it was so much more. I turned in my seat to look back at the empty sky. For fifteen years I had watched Earth wax from crescent to quarter to gibbous to full, and then wane to gibbous to crescent to new. I had watched her turn, continent, ocean, continent and ocean again. I'd seen the seasons change from cloud to clear, from southern summer to northern summer. But always the changing Earth had kept its position high above Kepler Crater, in the eastern sky, a little to the south. For fifteen years it had stared down at me, a huge blue eye, blinking open and shut. Eye-in-the-sky Earth.

Now, suddenly, it wasn't part of Moon's sky any more. I was on a new Moon, a private Moon, with no eye-in-the-sky, spy-in-the-sky. I felt free and light-headed, like someone leaving home to go out into the world and earn his living. Free, and at the same time afraid.

"Kep, what's the matter?" Ann's voice made me jump.

"Nothing." I turned and set off again westward. With neither sunlight nor earthshine the way ahead was dark. The searchlight of the camper threw a grey-white ellipse ahead of us, like scissors slashing through black velvet. Beyond it I could just see the dark curve of Moon's horizon, starlit against the overwhelming blackness of space.

We stopped twice for a snack of biscuit and a cup of hot synthoblend, but there was a terror in this dark silent world that crept closer when we were no longer moving, and I didn't need Ann's urging to get back to the controls.

Nothing seemed to change. One crater wall looked exactly like the one we had just passed. We might be going on for ever, I suddenly thought, creeping around the surface of Moon in eternal night, and, like the Flying Dutchman in the old Earth legend, never coming home to port.

"Kepler, look!" Her scared voice echoed my thoughts, and I pulled up abruptly and turned to follow her pointing arm.

Low in the southeastern sky Earth had suddenly looped up from below Moon's horizon. I got a dizzy sense of that *other* truth, that we were in fact two tiny creatures clinging to the surface of a great ball of silicon and basalt that wobbled and careened through space like a drunken top. Then everyday reality snapped back. My feet stayed *down*, where they belonged. *Up* was above us. Moon was solid and fixed in space, and out "there" everything else moved around it.

Earth dipped below the horizon. I knew, though I had never imagined that this is how it would look, that if we were to remain in this no-man's land between Earthbright and Earthdark, we would see Earth pop up and sink back in a series of complicated arcs like a yo-yo.

Ann laughed shakily. "That was something else! But I got a fix on it," she added practically. As we set out again she began to check the stars ahead against our position.

"What's that?" She pointed. "It's not the least bit familiar."

I stared. It wasn't. It shone, planet bright, high in the western sky

88

where no planet could be. I reached across for the binoculars. "It's got a visible disc, Ann," I said after a moment. "It's got to be a satellite."

"It can't be. We don't *have* any satellites. Space debris, perhaps?"

"Look for yourself." I handed her the glasses.

"It *is*. But how . . .?"

"It's in synchronous orbit above the centre of Earthdark. It'd never be seen from Earth, nor on the ferry runs. But who could have done it, and why the secrecy?"

"What's going on, Kep? A satellite over here, where nobody lives." Her voice changed and she stared at me.

I gripped her hand. "That's got to be the answer, Ann. There must be people living and working over here. Enough people to justify the expense of a communications satellite."

"But who? LEMCON? They've got the money. Colonists? No, that's crazy, it can't be *us*. We'd know about it."

"Unless it's a splinter group. Like the gillmen on Conshelf Ten. Not liking the political set-up, taking the law into their own hands."

"And Daddy? How does he fit in? It's ridiculous to think he could be a rebel. That must mean that someone's using him, doesn't it? LEMCON? Rebels? Oh, Kep, what do you think?" Her voice was sharp with fear.

I remembered how I had confronted Scarface at the door of Father's office, and how Father had lied about him. And Scarface was a LEMCON man. That I knew. "LEMCON, I think. It makes more sense."

"Oh, Kep, let's go on. Quickly!"

We drove west along the twentieth parallel. More or less. I knew how to navigate across the Ocean of Storms, where hundreds of miles of flat basalt overpour lay between the spatterings of more recent craters. It was different here. Here in Earthdark there were no *maria*; no supercollisions had flooded the moon surface with molten basalt. Here, since Moon was first a solid, the craters had been forming from meteorite impacts, touching each other, overlaying each other, as closely packed as the fruit in one of Aunt

Janet's cakes.

As I bumped and threaded my way between crater walls I longed for a world with a magnetic field, so that I could get a good compass bearing and stick to it.

Ann stayed glued to the map and the inertial navigator. By the time we had passed the hundredth degree of longitude she was pretty certain that we were no more than a couple of miles off course, either way.

Eighty miles further on and we figured we must have been sitting on top of it. Whatever *it* was.

We were in the rough interior plain of a huge crater, sixty or more miles across, bigger than Copernicus.

"What do you think?" I stretched and swivelled my chair to look at Ann.

"We located the other cave from the X on the map. Let's try it here. Look. Slap in the middle of the west wall." She pointed.

"I'll reconnoitre. If . . . well, if anything should go wrong, you could get the camper back home and tell them what's happened."

"Not on your life!" She scrambled out of her chair. "We go together, Kep, or not at all."

I looked at her face. Her jaw was set and her usually pale cheeks were flushed, Her dark eyes, well, there was a sparkle in them I'd never seen before. I put up my hands in mock surrender. "All right. You don't have to look as if you were going to eat me! We both go."

I cut the camper jets and coasted towards the western crater wall on battery power. We suited up in silence, and I switched off all the camper lights except for the signal that marked the air-lock entrance.

Ann's face told me nothing, but I know I felt very small and lonely as I stepped out into the black night of Earthdark. I left the outer hatch open behind us. It was a comfort to know we had a bolt-hole handy.

We stood close together, touching and yet apart, while our eyes grew accustomed to the dark and we got our bearings. Above our heads the Galaxy blazed, the fire of fifty billion stars chilled by the wastes of empty space.

To the west the stars were abruptly wiped out by a jagged line of darkness, less black than the blackness of space. The crater wall. We moved cautiously towards it on our jet-packs.

I switched on the intercom. Out here in Earthdark there was no one to eavesdrop. "Do you have your compass, Ann?"

My own voice sounded hollow inside my helmet. Ann's was warm and close to my ear. "Got it right here, Kep."

She skimmed ahead of me, watching the compass in her hand. Once she stopped, backtracked, then shook her head. We had traversed ten miles north along the crater wall before she stopped again. "Too far, I think, don't you? Let's try the other way."

She set off again, back along the broken slopes of the crater wall towards the place where we had parked the camper. The signal light above the entrance lock flashed a welcome on-off, on-off. We left it behind us, and went on in the darkness.

Ahead of me I could see the glow of Ann's jet-pack and the circle of light her flashlight made against the crater side. She slowed, hovered, switched off her jets and landed lightly on the flat of her moon-boots. The dust rose in a puff and settled again slowly, staining her silver boots with patches of brownish grey.

I landed beside her and looked over her shoulder. The compass needle pointed immovably at the crater wall ahead of us.

"Fantastic navigation! Twelve hundred miles right to the front door."

She made a mock bow, clumsy in her globe-like space helmet.

"And the front door is an air-lock."

"A new one too. Not one of the pioneer assemblies." I ran a gloved hand over the seal.

"But what's on the other side?" Her voice trembled. The moment of elation was over.

"We'll soon find out." I spun the huge wheel-type handle. It moved freely, so the lock was already at zero-atmosphere, and the heavy door swung slowly open. The light inside was dim, powered by solar batteries, I guessed, and in need of recharging in these last hours of darkness before the new day. I could see well enough to shut the outer hatch and find the controls to pump air into the lock.

It was a long two minutes before a buzzer announced that the pressure had equalised and I was able to swing the inner hatch open and peer into the passage beyond. Faint ceiling lights showed me a tunnel, no taller than a man, no wider than my outstretched arms, and perhaps eight or ten feet long. The natural moon rock had been smoothed down and sprayed with impermeable plastic spray. It gleamed palely in the glimmer of light. At its end was darkness.

I pushed up my face plate and cautiously sniffed the air. It was fresh and comfortably moist. "It's all right." I turned to help Ann with her space helmet, and in that moment the door behind us swung shut with a dull thunk. By *itself* the handle spun shut, and as we stood staring we heard the whine of the pump.

"Quick, Ann!" I leapt for the door. Together we tried to turn the handle. It was as immovable as moon rock. There were no controls on the outside of the hatch, no way of stopping that pump, or of opening the door.

The noise of the pump stopped. Ann pointed at the signal light above the hatch. It shone dully red. On our side of the door the atmospheric pressure stood at 14.7 pounds per square inch. On the other side it was as near zero as the pump could make it. The vacuum of space. Nothing and nobody was going to be able to open that door.

"Kep, we're trapped!"

Chapter Nine

I LIFTED OFF MY HELMET with hands that shook a little, and laid it carefully on the plastic-coated floor, before helping Ann with hers. In the dim light I could see how pale she was and how huge her dark eyes. I pulled off her gauntlets and tried to warm her hands.

"It's okay, Ann. It'll be all right."

She managed a weak smile. "You certainly know how to convince a girl. If you could see your face! Kep, what on Moon happened? How could the hatch shut and the pump start all by itself? Kep, how are we going to get out?"

"I wish I knew. But it didn't happen by accident. I mean, there are no exterior controls. So the door was meant to shut by itself the way it did. There's one thing about it." I tried to sound more cheerful. "Your navigation was certainly right on the button. Twelve hundred miles, door to door, so to speak. Look, that map was there for a good reason. I bet someone will come along soon to pick us up. That's it . . ." The more cheerful I sounded the more I began to believe myself. "I bet that's it, Ann. This is a rendezvous point. The door works that way so that someone can come in from outside and collect us. I bet if we'd noticed, there was a button inside the air-lock that would have kept the hatch open if we'd wanted it that way. Otherwise it automatically reverts to moon-atmosphere status."

Ann nodded. "That makes sense. Well, since we've got to wait, let's explore. I wonder if there's any food."

"Now there's a sound idea. Come on." I took her hand and together we walked along the narrow passage and around the bend,

93

talking cheerfully, each trying to keep up the other's spirits.

It was pitch dark in the cave beyond. That was the first surprise. I switched on my flashlight, but before I had time to register anything a brilliant glare blinded me. In the same instant the flashlight was twisted out of my hands. Beside me Ann cried out.

I turned. "Take your hands off her, you . . ."

"Naow, naow." The Australian drawl was soft in my ear. "You behave yourself, nipper, and I won't lay a hand on your sheila. But get any bright ideas . . ." He let the sentence hang there menacingly.

I swallowed and nodded. "All right. I won't try anything."

"Excellent." From across the room the fat man's voice came, as soft and smooth as cream. "Blue, turn on the lights. Harris, check the air-lock hatch." There was an urgent tone behind the smoothness. The overhead lights blinked on dimly, and the blinding light was moved away from my eyes.

I blinked and looked around. The cave was an average blowout. There were sleeping bags on the floor, a table and two chairs, and at the back, crates of stuff – food, I hoped. Beside the crates was the portable life-support system, which cleaned and re-cycled the air and kept the cave at a temperature a little cool, but perfectly liveable.

The fat man, Clint, faced us, the familiar gun in his hand. I put my arm round Ann and drew her close to me. Behind us Blue ran his hands over my moon-suit and then over Ann's. "They're not armed." He lounged across the cave to where Clint stood.

Footsteps sounded fast in the passage behind us. Clint and Blue looked past us, anxiously, it seemed, as the man called Harris entered the cave and brushed by.

"The hatch is closed." It was all he said, but the two men sagged. Blue swore under his breath. Clint's lips drew tight.

"You were on watch, Harris. Didn't you hear them come in? Or were you sleeping?"

Harris shook his head. "I heard nothing. The passage must act like a sound trap."

Clint slipped the gun into the front of his jacket. "So we meet again, young Masterman. You seem to bear a charmed life. I

94

wonder if your luck will continue to hold."

"Are you threatening me? My father knows that you tried to kill me before. If you try anything again, he knows where to look."

"Threaten? Me? No, my dear boy. This time we're all in the same boat – or I should say cave."

"What are you talking about?"

"This bleeding cave, duckie." The Australian's voice was high. "You can get in it easy, but you can't get out."

"You mean, it wasn't you who set the hatch to shut? Then who . . .?"

"That's the question, isn't it?"

"How did you get here anyway? Were you following us?"

"Following? Don't talk so soft. We've been here for hours already. We had a map."

"Shut up, Blue." The fat man's voice came soft and padded from his thin lips. "You talk too much. We'll ask the questions, young Masterman. How did you get here?"

"We had a map too." I pulled it from my knee pocket and handed it to Clint.

"Identical! Harris, what about it?" His eyes narrowed.

The man they called Harris shrugged. "That's the original, I suppose. The kids must have found it, where I did, in Dr Sheppard's room. I just photographed it and left it there. You know that."

I felt Ann quiver. She pushed away my encircling arm and leapt at the stranger with a yell that was pure animal. "You stole the map? From Daddy's room. Where is he? What have you done with him?"

It took the two of them to unhitch her from Harris. I was thankful that Clint had put away his gun. They pushed her, shaking and weeping, at me. "If you can't control her, I'll have her tied up," Clint said coldly. His eyes went back to Harris. "What's she talking about? Have you been double-crossing me?"

The man called Harris shook his head. He mopped at his left cheek with a handkerchief, and turned slightly so that I saw his face full on for the first time.

"Scarface!" I was so startled that I said it out loud. He looked at me bleakly, giving nothing away, dabbing at the bloody scratch across his lower cheek, that echoed the white and puckered scar running from his eye across to his cheekbone.

"Here." Blue pushed between us. "What's going on? You two know each other? You want to explain that, Harris. And what's all this about the sheila's father? Who *is* her old man?"

"He's Moon Comptroller, that's who he is. And this man . . ." Ann pointed a shaking hand at Scarface Harris. "This man must be the one who's kidnapped him. How else could he have got to photograph the map? It was hidden in his private sleeping room."

"Is that so." Blue's drawl became even more pronounced. "Naow what have you been up to, Jim Harris? Have you been doing yourself a bit of good on the side, kidnapping the Comptroller? Or perhaps you'd be on the same side, eh?"

"Don't be a bone-head, Blue. The girl's crazy. Why'd I want to kidnap the Comptroller? These kids are playing games, that's all."

"Dangerous games to bring them so far from home, alone." Clint's voice was space-ice. The gun was in his hand. Only this time it was pointing at Harris. "How interesting that young Masterman seems to recognise you. I wonder where you met?"

With some wild idea of helping ourselves by setting the LEMCON men at each other's throats I added fuel to the smouldering fire.

"Know him? Why, the last time I saw him he was talking with my father, in his private office, as friendly as could be."

I saw the muscles around Harris's neck and mouth tighten. That'll teach you, I thought savagely. Kidnapping Dr Sheppard and threatening my father . .

For such a heavy man Clint moved fast and Harris was caught unawares. The pistol butt came down sharply against the side of his head. Harris went down without a murmur. Ann screamed.

Clint tucked the gun away. "Tie him up, Blue. Tie him up well."

"We should finish him off right now."

"What? And have his body lying around in here with us? Use your head, Blue. Time for that later "

"What about these two?"

"What can they do? They're not going anywhere. They're

trapped as much as we are."

"He's slippery though, the boy. You should know. Made a fool of you, didn't he?" Blue grinned spitefully.

"That'll do." Clint's face was impassive. "But if he makes you nervous, tie the boy up. The girl . . . well, she can cook us a decent meal. If there's a way of making this moon grub eatable she should know it."

Blue dumped Harris at the back of the cave and tied my arms behind me to the frame of the life-support unit. By wriggling around a little I could see Harris's face. His eyes were shut and his skin was a dreadful clay colour. His lips had a line of blue around them. The wound behind his right ear was bleeding sluggishly. I began to feel sick. I'd done that, as surely as if I'd swung the pistol myself. Even if he had kidnapped Dr Sheppard, even if he'd intimidated my father. . . . Was he alive? If the wound was still bleeding it meant that he was still alive, didn't it?

Ann rummaged through the crates, pulling out cartons of food and reading the labels. Slowly she worked her way over until she was close to me. "Are you all right?" she whispered.

"Fine. Don't worry. Only my nose itches."

That made her smile. Then she looked down at Harris and grew grave again. "Is *he* dead?"

"I don't think so."

"Who are they? How did you know them? What's it all about?"

"LEMCON men. Be careful. I'll tell you later."

"I knew it. I wish I could poison them."

"Ann, don't even *think* like that. Don't provoke them. Do whatever they say. They'll stop at nothing. They tried to kill me before, in Aristarchus."

Her eyes widened. Then she turned and went on calmly sorting out supplies. Only I could see that her hands were shaking.

There was a hot-plate attached to the life-support unit and she cooked up a hi-protein meal for the men. When she handed it to them Blue swore horrendously and Clint said, "Take that muck away and bring us some real food."

"There's not much else, sir. We always use this for travel rations. It's very nourishing." Her voice trembled. "There's a can or two of meat. I could fry it and make instant scrambled eggs."

"That'll do. And lots of hot coffee."

"There's only syntho-blend." She sounded as if she was about to cry.

Clint only grunted, and Ann moved back to the hot-plate.

When she'd served them she said timidly, "The hi-pro cereal? May Kep and I have some? We're very hungry."

Clint nodded, and Blue laughed, his mouth full. "Pig swill. For pig colonists."

"Don't untie his hands." Clint looked at Ann with cold eyes. "You'll have to feed him yourself."

Ann brought over the bowls of hot meal and knelt down beside me. "Kep, I'm so sorry." Her eyes were full of tears.

"Don't be. This is no time to worry about dignity. Shove it in. I'm starving."

After she'd spoon-fed me she sat down on the floor of the cave between me and Harris and ate her own meal. I saw her hand go out and touch the unconscious man's neck. When Clint next looked up from his plate of fried meat and eggs she was scraping her bowl, as innocent as could be.

"Is he alive?" I whispered.

"I can feel his pulse. But hasn't he been unconscious an awfully long time? Suppose he's brain-damaged?"

I shrugged. I'd had the same idea, and pushed it out of my head. He'd threatened Father. I'd heard him. Maybe he'd kidnapped Dr Sheppard. Even if he were an enemy of Clint and Blue it didn't automatically make him a friend of mine. But I wished he would look less dead.

After our meal Ann sat close to me. Beside her Harris breathed heavily, almost snoring. Blue and Clint sat at the table near the cave entrance, playing cards.

The hours dragged by. Blue threw down his cards with a curse, and prowled the length of the tunnel and back, and around the perimeter of the cave. He examined every inch of the life-support unit. Ann shrank against me as he moved closer.

"We've looked, blockhead." Clint's voice was wearily impatient. "We've combed every inch. You know there's no way out."

"Are you going to sit there until we run out of air and water?" Blue flung back.

"There's enough for a month."

"And after that?"

"Smarten up, Blue. It's obvious this place is regularly used. Sooner or later someone is going to come by, and *this* time we'll be ready for them."

"Ruddy fink." Blue kicked Harris in the ribs, and slouched back to the table. I looked at Ann's watch and tried to wriggle into a more comfortable position. My arms were aching and my shoulder muscles were on fire.

Harris stopped snoring. We both looked down. His eyes were open, the strange eyes, one blue, one hazel. He licked his lips, painfully.

Quietly Ann got up and drew a glass of water and stood by the life-support unit while she sipped it. When she sat down she still had the glass. At the table Blue and Clint hunched over their cards.

Ann let some of the water trickle into Harris's mouth. He swallowed greedily and licked his lips again. They moved. One eye on the two men at the table, Ann leant close to him.

"He says he can help us get out," she turned and whispered to me.

I shook my head. He looked half-dead. What could he do to help? And why should he want to? What game was Scarface Harris playing now?

"Trust me." I couldn't hear the words, but I saw his lips move. Ann looked at me, her eyes begging.

I shrugged. After all, what had we got to lose? "Only don't untie him, whatever you do."

I saw her turn back to Harris and slide her hand into the front of his jacket, her eyes on Clint and Blue. A tiny bottle glinted in the palm of her hand. Harris whispered. Over Ann's shoulders I saw his lips ". . . in their next meal. Be sure not to eat any of it yourselves."

The bottle vanished into the cuff of Ann's space-suit. Harris lay with his eyes shut. Ann looked at her watch and stretched. Then she got up slowly and began to assemble another meal, some sort of freeze-dried stew, strictly Earth visitors' diet.

I didn't see the bottle leave her sleeve, but I saw it slide, empty, into the garbage container, before she carried the plates of stew across to Clint and Blue.

"Not bad at all." Blue sniffed the aroma. He caught Ann by the wrist. "You're a good little sheila. Pretty too. I could go for you. Skinny though. How about some *real* food, love." He speared a piece of meat and held it up in front of her face. "Come on now, duckie."

I saw Ann hesitate. Then she opened her mouth. I held my breath. Blue laughed, popped the meat into his own mouth and pushed her away. "Go and eat some of your pig swill. Go on."

I let my breath out slowly. I could see by the way she walked back across the cave that Ann was trying not to tremble. She stood by the hot-plate, her back to the men, and stirred up a mess of hi-pro cereal and brought the bowls over to where I was tied.

She fed me and then herself, keeping her eyes down on her bowl.

The room was very quiet. I could see Ann was finding it as hard to swallow the sticky synthetic meal as I had.

Cautiously I looked up. Blue's head was on the table, his long arms dangling to the floor. Clint was sitting hunched in on himself, like a big overstuffed bag of clothes.

"They'll be out for at least three hours." Harris's voice was weak, but matter-of-fact. "Untie me, there's a good girl, and give me some more of that water."

"No!" I shouted, and then looked uneasily at Clint and Blue. They didn't move. "Undo my wrists first, Ann, and then give him the water. But no untying, not till we know what's going on."

"You want to get out of here, don't you? Then untie me."

"What'll you do with us?"

"Take you to . . . to where you'll be safe."

"Oh, Kep!"

"Hold on, Ann." I stood up and rubbed my wrists. "Look, Mr Harris, those are fine words. But if you know how to get out, why didn't you go before?"

"With Clint and Blue there? After all the trouble I went to to lure them out here with the false map . . ."

"Huh?" I felt as if I were in free-fall. "False map?"

Ann pushed past me as I stood open-mouthed. She cut Harris's bonds and helped him sit up.

He groaned at the movement. "I've got to take something for this head or I'll be going off again. Get me the first aid kit."

I brought it over and stood there staring at him while he rummaged through it until he found what he wanted. He swallowed a pill with more water, and then got carefully to his feet.

"You should rest." Ann scolded him as he clutched at the life-support console for support.

He shook his head. "Ouch! Remind me not to do that again. No, there's no time. Kepler, help me into my space-suit. Come on. Hurry up."

He had one of the old-fashioned LEMCON suits and it took us a while to get it on to his satisfaction. Then he limped down the passage towards the air-lock, lifting Clint's gun from him as we passed. The fat man didn't even stir.

We stopped in front of the closed air-lock. Harris grinned faintly. "I shall now perform my celebrated 'Open Sesame' trick. Kepler, will you give the young lady a leg up so that she can reach the signal light above the hatch. That's right. Now, just above the light . . . you'll have to feel around for it . . . there's a small button. Got it? Now press it twice. And . . . open sesame."

Ann scrambled down as the air pump started. "It's working."

"You didn't believe me, did you? Come on kids, get on your helmets and gauntlets. We're going outside."

The door slid open and shut again behind us as we crowded in. It was a jam with the three of us and our jet-packs. "Wait." I put my hand over Harris's as he reached for the controls. "Tell us how it works. It doesn't make sense to build an air-lock that's a trap."

Harris smiled. "You'll get the idea that we're paranoid. But we had good reasons for building the locks this way. All right. If you press the *stop* button twice before starting the pump the air-lock works perfectly normally. Only for an intruder does it become a prison. Okay? All right. Visors down then." He punched the buttons.

I hesitated when we got out on to Moon surface again, but Harris pushed me firmly towards our camper. "I'll travel with you," he said, when we were inside again. "Less likely to cause alarm among the natives than if I turned up with you in a LEMCON carrier."

"Where is your vehicle?" I looked around. "I didn't see it when we arrived." Suddenly I was suspicious again.

"No reason why you should. I left it out there." Harris waved vaguely towards the dark of the crater centre. "I felt safer guiding those two thugs on foot, once they knew the right crater."

"If you didn't trust them why did you go with them? Why did you let yourself get trapped in the cave with them?"

"I never was trapped. Not till you blew my cover. I was just biding my time. Now let's stir. It'll be daylight soon and there's work to do."

He had me make an ice-pack by dipping a wad of cloth into some of our drinking water and then taking it outside the camper for a second. When Ann had bound it into a compress on the swelling behind his ear he said it was much more comfortable. He thanked her with a charming smile that didn't go at all with his strange-coloured eyes and his villainous scar.

I was all mixed-up about Harris. I found myself liking him, and then I would see the LEMCON space-suit and right away the anger would be hot in my throat.

Ann seemed to have no such problem. As she bound up his head she touched the weal on his cheek where she'd scratched him. "I'm really sorry, Mr Harris. I was wrong. You didn't kidnap my father, did you?"

"No, Miss Sheppard, I didn't. I wasn't even in his room. But don't worry about it. I understand."

Then she said he should call her Ann, and pretty soon they were so cosy that I got mad all over again and burst out. "Well, I'm still not satisfied. What were you doing in Aristarchus? And in my father's office? And how did you get the map if you weren't in Dr Sheppard's room?"

"Whoa! Calm down. It's complicated enough. Too bad you saw me that day in Aristarchus. It really confused things. You see I represent the more conservative LEMCON investors on Earth. The ones that disapprove of some of the strong arm tactics that have been used. They sent me up to find out what's been going on."

"And the other faction hired Clint and Blue?"

"Clint anyway. Blue's just a roughneck Clint has to do his running for him. Your coming on the scene that day in Aristarchus sort of precipitated things. I had to ask your father for help to trap the two of them away from Aristarchus. The last thing we needed was to have the miners rioting. He gave me the map . . . or rather a copy of it . . . it's perfectly genuine, by the way, but nothing, as they say, to do with the case."

"Then how did the original map get into Dr Sheppard's room? And why was it hidden like that if it wasn't important?"

He laughed. "A competent spy covers all possibilities. I didn't know . . . I still don't know . . . if Clint's organisation has someone inside Kepler Base. I said I found the original map hidden in Dr Sheppard's room, so that's where it had to be. Insurance. That's all. Your father hid it for me, Kepler. Neither of us expected you two enterprising kids to re-find it!"

I felt myself getting red all the way up my neck and into my ears. "You mean we followed a phony map all the way across the Ocean of Storms into Earthdark for *nothing*?"

"I'm afraid so." His face was serious, though there was a twinkle in the strange eyes. "Look, don't take it too hard. After all, the map fooled a hard-boiled professional like Clint, didn't it?"

That cheered me up a bit. He really was a good sort.

"What happens to us now? Are you taking us all the way back to Kepler Base?"

"'After I've brought you out so far, And made you trot so quick'" he quoted. "That would be an anticlimax, wouldn't it? No, I don't think so. I don't really have the time. But I'll have to check the alternative over the radio. Excuse me." He pushed past our knees into the driving compartment.

I dived after him. "Look, you can't mess about with my equipment," I blurted out, and he looked up from the dials, a smile crinkling the corners of his eyes.

"You're still not quite convinced that we're on the same side, are you?"

"No, I guess not. You see, when you were in my father's office I heard you threaten him."

"Threaten?"

I told him I'd heard his last words as he'd charged out of Father's office the watch before Ann and I left for Earthdark.

He stared at me blankly and then roared with laughter. "Ouch! My head. Kepler, I'm sorry, but that's still another misunderstanding. You heard . . . what was it? . . . 'If you don't, Dr Sheppard'll be for it.' . . . and you took it for granted that I was the kidnapper and I was threatening your father? Oh, dear!"

I gulped. He patted my shoulder. "It's an easy mistake to have made, after what Ann had just put in your head. You see I'd just been telling your father that Clint was getting too close to Moon colony's plans . . . that's Dr Sheppard's organisation. I told the Governor how necessary it was for me to get Clint and Blue out of the way. He'd just given me the copy of the map. That must have been what you heard." I still couldn't say anything. He went on. "Anyway, Kepler, I think you and Ann are two blinking marvels to keep all this to yourselves and drive half way round Moon on a do-or-die rescue mission. You deserve a medal for it."

"But it was all unnecessary. I feel such an idiot."

"It's the thought that counts," said Harris vaguely, fiddling with the radio controls.

I watched him. "That thing's useless in Earthdark," I reminded him. "You can tune till you're blue. There's nothing to bounce the signals off."

"You want to bet." A squeal from the radio made a liar out of me. He grinned. "You've forgotten our satellite." He pointed up through the view-screen. "It's in synchronous orbit above the centre of Earthdark, just like Earth on the other side."

Our satellite, he'd said. I stared at him, new questions stirring in my mind. *Ours.*

He plugged in the headset, so I could only hear his half of the conversation. "Hallo, Gen One, this is Loner. May I bring in a couple of visitors? . . . No, not them. They're sleeping peacefully as arranged . . . Yes. Kepler Masterman and Ann Sheppard . . . Yes, that's what I said . . . I'll drop them off. Goodbye Gen One." He unplugged the headset and switched off. "All right if I drive, Kepler?" He turned to me. "I know the way in blind from here."

I nodded, feeling completely out of my depth, and went back to sit with Ann in the sleeping compartment.

"What's happening?" She finished tidying away the first-aid stuff.

I shrugged. "Don't ask. But he's part of whichever outfit put that satellite up in space. They must live over here. It's not LEMCON anyway," I added. "At least I don't think so."

"Of course not. I could have told you that. He's a very nice man."

I nearly reminded her that she had attacked the very nice man tooth and nail no more than five hours earlier, but then I decided that there was no reason for two of us to feel stupid. So I said nothing, and Ann broke the silence. "Where are we going?"

I laughed rather bitterly. "I wish I knew. The whole thing's got a bit out of hand, hasn't it? All that hero stuff, riding in to rescue your father from perils unknown . . . now I don't even know where we're going."

She put her hand on my arm. "Kep, I'll never forget what you did for me. Even though it seems that Daddy doesn't need rescuing I'm glad we did it. I've got to know you, away from the others, away from the Base, and . . . well, I'm glad, that's all."

I sat in the glow of that, thinking how odd fate was, for I too had found depths in Ann that I'd never have suspected back on Kepler Base.

"Nearly there." Harris's voice interrupted our thoughts. "Time to suit up."

We were standing ready by the air-lock when he came through. "What about you? Aren't you coming?"

He lounged in the doorway between the two compartments. "No. Here's where our ways part. There's an air-lock in the crater wall right in front of you. Follow the passage and you'll find another lock at the other end. Don't forget the way I told you to operate them. Goodbye, kids."

"You sound final. Won't we ever see you again?" Ann asked.

"I'd be surprised if our paths ever crossed again. I'm going down to Earth to report to my bosses. Don't know where my next assignment will take me, but it won't be Moon. Now off with you. Good luck, kids." He turned abruptly. It seemed to me that his face twisted suddenly, beneath the tortuous scar.

Ann and I locked through on to moon surface. It was still dark, but far above our head the crater rim glowed with points of fire. It was almost another dawn.

The lock in the crater wall was a duplicate of the one behind which we had been prisoners, only now we knew its secret and moved swiftly through to the passage beyond. It was a long walk downhill, long enough, I guessed, to bring us up clear inside the crater rim.

"Will we be coming out on to moon surface again?" I asked Ann. "Is that why there are two locks?"

"I think it's like the drawbridge across the moat, to keep out intruders," she said softly. "The other side . . . maybe an enchanted castle?"

And in a mood of wonder we locked through to a vestibule with earth-atmosphere. We stripped off our helmets and gauntlets. And unsealed our moon-suits. It was very warm. Almost hot.

The air was very moist and smelt strange, like . . . what was it?

"It smells just like Earth!" Ann ran ahead of me, out into the *open*.

"Ann, come back!"

"Oh, Kep!" She turned, her eyes shining as I had never seen them shine before. "Kep, it *is* magic. Come and look."

Beyond the entrance was a mass of greenery, vining and twisting up under the low moon-grav towards a silvery domed sky, shadowy distant beyond a lattice-work of arc-lights far above our heads.

In front of us, and to right and left, and along every diagonal the plants grew in precise ranks, their green leaves huge, umbrellas

106

spread open to the light, collapsed into a rib-work of veins where the shadows fell. Many of them bore flowers and I noticed that some of them were already fruiting, great bean-like pods that hung heavily from the vines even in moon gravity.

I looked up. "Ann, what's keeping it out?"

"Keeping what out?"

"Space."

"What a funny way to put it, Kep. I was just thinking how clever it was of them to keep the air in. Smell it. Isn't it wonderful? Real plant oxygen. There's a dome up there. You can just see where the sun catches the top. It must be aluminised plastic. Yes, look, right behind us, against the crater wall, you can see where it's fastened down."

"Plastic *film*? Against *meteorites*? It's insane. Sooner or later it's bound to go. Just like a bubble." I felt sick at the thought, sick and naked.

"What's the matter with you, Kep? It's wonderful. Like Earth, only not dirty and overcrowded. Oh!" She had bumped into a figure that had come hurrying down one of the green aisles that seemed to radiate from the air-lock entrance.

He wore standard colony uniform. I stared. "Tim O'Connor!" Tim, the most liked and trusted pilot in Moon. "Tim, what are *you* doing here?"

"Oh, just a spot of moon-lighting, me boy-oh! And I might ask the same of you two. Properly set the cat among the pigeons, you have. Anyway, welcome to Genesis. You're to come with me, both of you. The Boss wants to see you. Oh, put these on your belts. You'll need them while you're here."

"What is it?" I looked curiously at the small plastic cube Tim handed me. I'd seen one like it before . . .

"It's a nullifier. Clip them to your belts and don't go out without them or you'll wake up with a hang-over."

That was familiar too. "What do they nullify? Oh, come on, Tim!"

He shrugged. "They'll be telling you all of it, I suppose, or you wouldn't have been let through. We've put up an energy layer above the dome to repel meteorites and filter the ultra-violet. Like a force-field, you see? It works jim-dandy, only it knocks people out too. Carry your nullifier and everything in the garden's lovely again. See?"

I saw, and remembered where I'd seen them before. In Aristarchus. On Clint and Blue. My head was buzzing with the implications. Distantly I could hear Ann's excited voice. "Talking of gardens, how long has this one been going on for, Tim? And why all the secrecy?"

"Five years from start to finish. The rest, well, I expect the Boss will want to do all the explaining."

The Boss? Again the shadowy fears that lurked around the corners of my mind began to gather together and creep forward. If LEMCON wasn't running this place, then who was? A rival Earth group? Or a bunch of rebel colonists? And how did Clint and Blue get the nullifiers?

Above all who *was* the Boss? And *what* was Genesis?

Chapter Ten

TIM LED US OUT into the magical green world. After a time the vines were replaced by a springy ground cover like heather. In the centre of the more open area was a collection of buildings.

I was disappointed. I suppose that after our dramatic entrance through the tunnel into the magic moon garden I had been expecting something more fantastical and science-fiction, with elegant spires and decorated towers and slim flying buttresses.

In fact the buildings were nothing more than a collection of a dozen cannibalised fuel-tanks, half-sunk into the crater bottom, and floored to provide each sphere with a large dome-ceilinged room above, another room beneath, and curved storage space below that again.

"Follow me." Tim entered one of the open doors. Doors, open to the sky, I thought wonderingly, and ducked thankfully inside. If anything did rupture that plastic dome I would be just as dead, but I felt less naked inside the buildings.

Tim led us in silence down a spiral flight of stairs and through several rooms filled with packing cases, or rigged up as offices and labs. Whatever operation was going on out here in Earthdark it was certainly *big*. Up another staircase to a closed door. Tim knocked and, in the pause that followed, my mind ran madly to and fro deciding what to do, what I should say. Which I couldn't know until I finally saw who the Boss was.

"Come in," a voice answered the knock.

Tim pushed open the door. "They're here," he said, and left us on the threshold.

"Well, Ann, Kep! You *have* been busy, haven't you?"

"Daddy, Daddy!" Ann hurled herself at him and threw her arms round his neck. I just stood there with my mouth hanging open. A small part of my mind regretted that Ann had never got that emotional about me. The rest of my mind was one enormous question mark.

Dr Sheppard unhitched Ann gently. "Sit down, both of you, and tell me how in thunderation you got here."

There was an awkward pause, and then we both started talking at once. Finally, in bits and pieces, with devastating questions at intervals, he got the complete story out of us. It sounded even sillier than it had when I'd told it to Scarface Harris.

When we were through Huntley Sheppard looked at us from under his shaggy eyebrows. "Aye. Well, I'm blessed if I know whether to have you two shot at dawn for breaking every rule in the book, or to pin a couple of medals on you for what you were trying to do."

"You never were in danger, were you, Daddy?" Ann said in a very small voice.

"No, my very dear foolish girl. Only of losing my mind at the exploits of my only and previously level-headed daughter."

Ann blushed. "I'm sorry. But Daddy, *why* did you vanish like that? You'd never done it before. I was so worried . . . and nobody'd tell me anything . . ."

"I'm sorry, pet. The few people who did know where I was were sworn to total secrecy. I'd always had time to cover my tracks when I went away before, but this time it was a crisis and I left literally at a moment's notice . . . in fact the moment after you got back from Aristarchus, Kepler, and dropped that bombshell on your father."

"Bombshell? Me?" I stared.

"Yes, you. When you told your father that someone in LEMCON had the Genesis repeller and the nullifier it told him that there was a LEMCON spy right here in Genesis. I had to get out here right away in person, since there was no safe way of communicating between Kepler Base and Earthdark . . . anyone could have overheard, in LEMCON or back on Earth. So I had to come."

"You're the Boss?" I stared.

"Aye."

"And Father . . . he knows all about this . . . Genesis thing?" My mouth was suddenly dry.

"But of course he . . . Kepler, what kind of operation do you think we're running out here?" His eyes pierced me.

I exploded. "Well, sir, the whole thing's been so wrapped in secrecy I don't know what we thought. At first LEMCON, then we decided that maybe you were a rebel group from Moon colony."

"Good grief, what a vote of confidence! First, I'm a helpless kid-nappee and then I'm boss of a criminal operation. Listen you two chumps. Genesis is *ours*. Moon colony's. Yours and mine."

"Why so much secrecy?" I thought Ann was going to burst into tears. "This nightmare we've been through need never have hap-pened if you'd only trusted us."

"I'm really sorry, pet. But we couldn't tell you. Genesis has been five slow patient years in the building. Your father picked me to run it. It's been my chief assignment on Moon, with a new com-puter handling most of the regular Comptroller's work. Secrecy was the keynote from the first. If LEMCON had found out what we were up to they would certainly have sabotaged us."

"Why?" I interrupted.

"Our success would be their loss, and the stakes are huge, Earth's petrodollar investment, no less. Our scientists were involved on a need-to-know basis only, and sworn to total secrecy. Our security seemed to be air-tight, until Kepler came back from Aristarchus and exploded that bombshell."

"Have you found the spy who stole the repeller?"

"No. It's a serious concern, but not as bad as it could have been. We've been able to do the next best thing, to complete the Gen-esis project a month ahead of schedule. This solar dawn your father is going to notify the UN of LEMCON's treaty violations and ask them to send up an inspection team at once. We will then be able to show them Genesis One as a functioning unit and demand total independence." He leaned back in his chair and beamed.

"But what actually *is* Genesis? The dome? The plants?"

"That and much more. It's our bid for independence. We know that if LEMCON pulls out of Moon, much of Earth's interest in supporting Moon colony goes with it. We could have found ourselves stranded up here without resources.''

"Clint said as much to Blue,'' I remembered out loud.

"Can Moon really be self-sufficient?'' Ann asked.

"It's already happening. Now we can produce enough water, oxygen and food to support a growing population the rest will follow. We began five years ago with the satellite and the dome, communications and shelter. Then the patient development of new strains of plants, high in both food value and oxygen production. And water. Already we've developed new methods of water extraction from ore much less wasteful than LEMCON's, using the heat of day, cold of night contrast of the terminator zone. And we've discovered ice down under the south polar mountains, a hundred years' supply of it. By the time it's used up we'll have found new ways, maybe by artificially increasing Moon's mass so that it will hold an atmosphere. Then we can develop a true ecology. Who knows what's possible? Look how far we've come since 1969!''

"Daddy, it's thrilling. I'm proud to be a part of it. If only you could have told us. Oh, but don't send us straight back. Give us time to look around. Please?''

"You shouldn't be here at all. But . . . oh, very well. I'll get Tim to show you the ropes. A couple of days, no more, mind, and keep out of people's way.''

"Just one last thing, Dr Sheppard.'' I hung back in the doorway. "Clint and Blue? What'll happen to them?''

"Among other things they'll be tried back on Earth for attempted murder — yours. I still wish I knew how they got the repeller. I wouldn't have thought they had the brains.''

"They called it an inhibitor.'' I remembered.

"That's what I mean. Stupid men. How could they get close enough to Genesis to steal the repeller and yet not even understand its use? It could have been invaluable to LEMCON. But to exploit its damaging side-effect and ignore its real potential — only a basically stupid man would do that.'' He shook his head disgustedly.

"And Scarface? I mean Harris. What do you suppose will become of him?''

"He'll be on his way back to Earth with Clint and Blue. It proves LEMCON's not all bad, doesn't it? The shareholders hiring a man like that to find out what's going on in its own operation. I never did meet Harris personally, and I think your father only saw him a couple of times, but he thought him quite a character. And clever. Smart as a whip. And cool. That was a neat trap he set for those two thugs."

"And for us too, it turned out." I smiled ruefully.

"Well, it's over now, dear boy. You won't make the same mistake twice. Now off with you. I've work to do."

For the next two days we wandered around Genesis colony, at first guided by Tim O'Connor, and then on our own. The dome covered the whole floor of the ten-mile diameter crater, and could easily have held a small city and still have a large enough green belt for food and oxygen, so there was plenty to see.

The heavy equipment and the water-processing terminator crawlers were parked out on Moon surface and serviced there. Inside Genesis were no machines. For people in a hurry there were wide-tyred bicycles. It was quiet and clean, and once I became accustomed to the naked feeling of being outdoors without a moonsuit I loved it. It had the same quality of freedom that life under the sea had had.

"I'd like to spend my life here," I confessed to Ann, as we walked together along the dense ranks of sweet-smelling soy-vine.

"I asked Father about the possibility," she admitted. "He said, not till we're twenty and have our degrees. There's so much work still to be done, and they can only afford to carry experienced personnel. There's another catch too."

"A catch?"

"They're only colonising the Genesis cities with married couples." Her cheeks were suddenly charmingly pink.

I laughed. "Well, how about it, Ann? Are those lectures on Celestial Mechanics back in 'B' Watch too hot to miss? Or would you consider transferring back to 'A'?"

"Kep, you beast! You know I only transferred to get some breathing space. When you got back from those three months on

113

Earth you were so . . . oh, dear, you were impossible. I didn't know how I was going to *bear* being married to you."

"And now what do you think?"

"You're different. Nice different."

I put my arm round her and kissed the tip of her nose. "You too. Nice different."

We must have walked for an hour through the jungle growth without paying any attention to where we were going. Not that it mattered. The sun had dawned two days before, and we could see its glow through the luminised plastic of the dome, low above the eastern horizon. We just had to keep that glow to our right and sooner or later we'd find our way back to the huddle of temporary buildings at the centre of Genesis One colony.

We turned back and strolled slowly along the green-leaved tunnels in a happy trance, wanting nothing more out of life than what we had at that moment.

Then, "Look, Kep. Just to our right. A clearing and a building. I wonder what it is?"

"Want to look?"

"Mmm. Let's."

It turned out to be only an instrument shack, open front and rear, probably a protection against the sun or the irrigating mists that periodically watered the vines. There was nobody there, though an open log book, half filled with neat figures, lay upon one of the consoles.

"Well, that's not too exciting. Shall we go on? It must be nearly lunch-time and I'm starving."

"You're always starving." Ann laughed and swung my arm to and fro.

We bumped into him in the doorway. Head-on. Anywhere else we'd never have given him a second glance. Anywhere else he'd have had time to control his reactions on seeing us again.

He was such an ordinary-looking man, in standard colony coveralls, with short mouse-coloured hair and washed-out blue eyes. He was about my height, but then I'm tall for my age. Came of being born under moon-grav, the doctors said. His face was the kind you simply don't remember. Medium nose. Medium mouth.

Medium chin. No wrinkles. No moles. Nothing to catch the eye except the nasty scratch low down on his left cheek. It was red and a little puffy as if it were infected.

I drew back with a muttered "excuse me", but Ann just went on standing there, staring up into his face as if she'd just seen a snake.

His reaction was just as odd. His face blanched. I could actually see how the blood drained from it so that the scratch in contrast stood out crimson. His face sharpened. I could see his cheekbones and the hollows in his temples. Still staring back at Ann his left hand went slowly up and covered his cheek.

All this couldn't have taken more than ten seconds, though it seemed to run for ever in a dream-like slow motion.

Ann recovered first. "It *is* you. I'd know that scratch anywhere. It *did* get infected. You should put something on it or it'll take ages to heal. But . . ." she frowned up at the face a foot away from her own. "What's happened? Why are you here? And where's that terrible scar? I don't understand. And your eyes. One eye was hazel, wasn't it, Kep?" She turned to me as the man's hand went up in a hatchet chop.

I yanked her arm and spun her behind me as the murderous hand came down. He'd made a fast recovery from the shock. Why had I thought his eyes were weak? There was a light in them now as cold as space itself. As lonely and dangerous.

"Run, Ann. Get help quickly. Go on. Run, I tell you."

I daren't look behind me. I kept myself between Harris and her retreat, weaving from left to right, and then, after a moment I backed slowly down the room, dodging those hands.

At last I was in the open, running north towards the settlement. Ann was out of sight. She must have taken another path. I loped along the green tunnel that a moment before had seemed like the entrance to paradise. Now it was a trap. Harris's feet were heavy behind me. Closer. Closer yet. I flung myself to one side and he thundered by, arms flailing as he tried to stop himself.

He was much faster on his feet than I was, I realised, but he was relatively new to moon-grav and clumsy at changing speed and direction. If I wanted to come out of this with a whole skin I should have to fight on my terms, not his.

Time was what I needed desperately. Time for Ann to get to the buildings and bring back help. How far away were we? How soon? Twenty minutes? More? How could I possibly keep Scarface at arm's length for that long?

I had a hazy idea that if I could only distract him, get him to talk about himself, maybe I could spin out the time a little longer. Anyway, it was a ploy that always worked in detective novels.

We faced each other again, dodging and weaving. There was a smile on Harris's face now, a small self-confident smile. Was that a strength or a weakness?

"I don't understand, Harris. I thought you'd gone back to Earth?"

"Earth? My home's here. In Genesis. And my name's not Harris. You've made a mistake." He grinned and his hand slashed down. I wondered where he had learned his fighting. I sprang backwards and his fingers just grazed the front of my coveralls. Too close by far.

"How could you have been in Genesis all this time?" I panted. "*And* in Aristarchus?"

"It wasn't easy. But I'm known as a loner. It's possible to fake check-ins if you know the ropes. I could be out working in Earthdark and back in Aristarchus all at the same time." He came at me with a rush, and I ducked under his arm and faced him from behind. He whirled. His smile didn't look so pleasant now. We fought in silence for a time. Then,

"It was *you* who stole the secret of the repeller field!"

"Of course. That was my 'in' with Clint. I told him I'd come up from LEMCON headquarters to instal it and keep tabs on the miners. When he'd seen how it worked he lapped up whatever I told him after that." He moved to one side. I mirrored his move.

We talked on, when we had breath enough, our eyes on each other's eyes, our feet always moving, retreating, advancing, like some strange outmoded dance.

"But if you're working for LEMCON why did you put a stop to Clint and Blue?"

Harris laughed shortly. "Clint was getting too close to me,

116

and after their stupid attempt to kill you I decided they were expendable."

"But if they're to stand trial back on Earth they can still talk."

"Not them. They never got there. Didn't you know? An unfortunate accident. Something must have gone wrong with the air-lock. By the time I got back to the cave there was no atmosphere. Pity." He shook his head. "Still, it must have been a very peaceful end. They never felt a thing."

I choked. And Ann and I had helped him do it. We'd given Clint and Blue the drug. We had untied Harris. And now I knew for certain that there was no way he was going to let me live. His past had to die and I was part of that past.

He must have read it in my eyes. "Quite right, dear boy. It never pays to be nosy."

I mustn't run, I told my legs. Fight on my terms, not on his. I managed a smile and saw the reluctant admiration in his face. "What can you hope to gain by staying in Genesis now? It's complete. You've lost. The UN team will be here by midnight. You can't spoil things any more."

"Spoil things?" His voice was hurt. "Why should I want to spoil things? You misunderstand my motives entirely. I never did want to spoil Genesis. The firm I work for only wants to help. LEMCON's through. That's been plain for quite a while. The firm wishes to reinvest in something more, how shall I say, long term. Genesis has a future. We have a great deal of money and we shall be happy to help that future happen."

"Mafia money? Or is it petrodollars?" I gasped. The stitch in my side was getting difficult to ignore. "Either way we don't want it. We don't want your money, nor the control that goes with it. We don't need it."

"Oh, but you see, that's my job. To establish the need." His voice was honey-sweet. "You'd be surprised just how much Moon is going to need our money. We'll make sure of that. You can count on it."

"You rotten beast. People like you . . . they spoil everything." I forgot all my strategy and went for him in a rush. I got in too close for him to disable me with a karate chop, but I felt a rib go before I

117

was able to break free of his squeeze.

I stood back, fighting the pain. He made a sudden grab. I jumped back, but not fast enough nor far enough. He snatched the nullifier from my belt and hurled it high among the vines.

I saw the plastic cube turning corner over corner, pausing, and then falling, bouncing from leaf to leaf. There was no way I could tell where it had landed. I could hunt for an hour and never find it.

Harris had turned his back on me and was running down the aisle of vines away from the Genesis buildings. I couldn't believe my luck. He was going to let me live!

Then he stopped, a hundred yards away and turned to watch me. I realised, with a sudden lurch in my gut, that without the nullifier I would be unconscious in less than five minutes. He could wait in safety, watch me go down and then stroll back and finish me off without even leaving a bruise.

Once the scratch on his face had healed could Ann ever identify him? She'd seen him without the scar and the hazel-eye contact lens for only a few seconds. With me it was different. When you've looked into a man's eyes and seen your own death mirrored there you don't forget him. Not ever. Only, without my nullifier, it looked as if "ever" was going to be a very short time indeed.

If I ran towards Harris he had only to retreat another hundred yards, drawing me farther and farther away from rescue. . . .

I ran a couple of steps towards him, and as he turned his back on me I dived through the tangle of vines into the next aisle. I heard his footsteps stop, and began to move as fast and as softly as I knew how. I could imagine him standing there, puzzled. Wondering where I was.

My head was beginning to spin and I staggered, brushing against the great leaves. I froze. I heard his footsteps coming towards me, Earth-heavy on the crushed lava dirt. I held myself very still, breathing steadily, willing myself back to strength.

It worked. My head began to clear and I could see again. He must be standing very close to me now, his nullifier protecting both of us from the effect of the force-field above the dome.

I could almost *hear* him listening, standing on the balls of his feet, hands rigid, ready to run and strike. Separated from him only by the screen of green leaves I stood lightly, relaxed, trying to breathe evenly, pushing away the pain of my broken rib.

Every minute was in my favour. Every minute my head grew clearer. If I could only match his moves for a little longer, stay within the protection of his nullifier, play cat and mouse until my rescuers got here. How long would it be before he realised what I was up to?

His footsteps moved, back towards the place where he had left me. I moved too, lightly, lightly. He stopped. He was getting edgy. I could *feel* the vibrations of his unease. He moved again. Only a few steps this time. I didn't budge. He listened. I waited.

Then he was off, briskly, as if he'd made up his mind. I padded along on the other side of the screen of vines. Soon he would be bound to see the hole in the vines I had made when I had burst through. Then he would see me. And he wouldn't let me play the same game twice.

I had two choices. I could run as far as I could and hide among the vines before the repeller field knocked me out, hoping that Ann's rescue team found me before Harris did. Or I could stay and fight, try and grab *his* nullifier and disable him.

Under the sea they had taught me never to turn my back on a predator fish. I'd stick with that advice now. I flattened myself against the leaves, right beside the tattered hole I'd made in my blind jump through the vines. I willed myself into stillness, into not breathing, almost into not being.

And waited.

He came through in a rush, crouching, hands slashing. A hair behind the reach of those murderous hands I snatched for his nullifier, grasped it and threw it, high, high, almost to the dome roof.

Then I was down, his knee on my chest, his hands on my throat. I struggled until I couldn't see any more, and then I let the repeller field swirl me away on a swift tide of unconsciousness.

Chapter Eleven

WHEN I WOKE UP properly again, stiff as a mummy in bandages from armpit to waist, and with the sore throat of a lifetime, I was back underground. Kepler Base, I recognised lazily . . . the hospital.

Father was there, looking anxious. "Did you get Harris?" I managed to whisper. Talking was an agony.

He nodded and smiled, his hands over one of mine. "Thanks to you, Kep. I'm proud of you."

"He was your spy."

"I know."

". . . killed Clint, Blue. He told me."

"We found them. We thought that's what had happened. Don't talk any more, Kep. It's all over. Moon is safe."

"Ann?"

"You'll see her soon. Now sleep. That's an order."

So I did.

Three weeks later, at midnight, when Earth was a huge silver dollar in the sky, the UN team arrived. I was with Father when the final decisions were made, LEMCON was wound up and Moon took her first proud step along the road towards independence.

"No hard feelings, I hope." Father shook hands with Miles Fargo when it was all signed and sealed.

Fargo tried to smile. "Hard feelings? No. We had a run for our money. But I have to worry about what's going to become of my boys now you colonists are taking over the mines."

"I could use some experienced miners." Father rubbed his chin thoughtfully.

"They're good all right. The best. But the devil to handle, I warn you."

"Not if you give them decent quarters and let them bring their families up here."

"It'll cost you a fortune."

"It could be cheaper in the long run if it makes the miners happy. Anyway, we're lucky. We don't have to answer to those shareholders of yours, so we can make independent decisions. Tell you what, Miles. Why don't *you* keep the mines going? The colony will set the prices fair and square, pay you a salary and distribute the minerals back on Earth on a 'need', not a 'want' basis."

"You'll never get rich that way, Governor. Nor will I. No thanks."

"I've an additional proposition, Miles, if you change your mind and go along with the first one." Father reached into a drawer and brought out a small box. When he opened it the whole room seemed to catch fire.

Miles drew a deep breath. "Oh, you beauty." He picked up the gem between finger and thumb. "What is it?"

The room danced with ruby and sapphire. At the heart of the stone was a glow like that of a comet in deep space.

"What is it?" Father repeated Miles Fargo's question. "It hasn't been given a name yet. I could tell you it's chemical composition, but I don't suppose you care. But what will interest you is that we've found quantities of these beauties over in Earthdark. Why don't *you* name it."

"Do I get to market it?" Fargo's hand closed over the fiery gem.

"If you buy the rest of my deal. And I don't care what outrageous amount you charge for it. Whatever the traffic will bear. These are for the 'want' budgets, not for the 'needs'."

"All right, Governor, you're on. I'll run the mines your way. You arrange the exporting and set the prices, except for the firestone. I have sole rights to it."

"Done."

They shook hands on it, and Miles Fargo hurried out, the box clutched in his hand.

"Miles!"

"Yes, Governor?" He turned at the door.

"Just one thing. I'd like you to arrange to have a dozen stones, a matched set, to be made up into a necklace for my daughter-in-law."

Miles Fargo grinned. "You shall have it, Governor."

When Father and I were alone he said quietly. "I hope I wasn't out of line then, Kep."

"No, Father, not at all. Everything is going to be all right for Ann and me now."

"No second thoughts about going back to Conshelf Ten?"

"Oh, I've thought about it. Quite a lot recently. I suppose it will always be a very special memory. But no. There's lots of work for us to do in Earthdark. A whole future. I don't think I'll ever go back. But one day, perhaps, one of our children . . ."

Also by Monica Hughes in Mammoth

CRISIS ON CONSHELF TEN

When Kepler Masterman visits Earth for the first
time, he finds heavy gravity impossible to live in. An
underwater atmosphere seems to offer the best solu-
tion to his problems, and friendly relatives welcome
him to their experimental community under the
ocean, many fathoms deep. But on Conshelf Ten
Kepler discovers a sinister situation linked to the
mysterious, water-breathing Gillmen, and realizes
that not only is he in great personal danger but the
survival of the entire Earth is threatened.

'Strangely convincing'   *Daily Telegraph*

'An excellent story'   *The Times*

THE TOMORROW CITY

A computer – C-Three – the brainchild of Caro's
father, is programmed to cater for the needs of every
man, woman and child in Thompsonville. Under its
benevolent control there would be no more dirt and
rubbish, no more dilapidated houses, no traffic jams.
'The city belongs to the children,' said Caro's father.
But gradually Caro and her friend David begin to
realise with increasing alarm that *they* belong to C-
Three. With the entire population subjected to mass
mind-control and mesmerised by television, Caro and
David decide C-Three must be stopped at all costs –
even if they have to stake their lives against its seeming
indestructibility.

The Keeper of the Isis Light

When a group of settlers from Earth land on the beautiful planet of Isis they arrive to a world completely uninhabited except by Olwen, Keeper of the Isis Light and her protector, Guardian. Olwen is nervous about what the newcomers will think of her and frustrated when she must put on a germ-free suit before she descends to the valley where they are camped. But Mark London quickly befriends the masked Olwen and she discovers the pleasures and pains of human friendship. And ultimately she learns why she and this alien planet are uniquely linked.

The Guardian of Isis

Jody is forced to leave the primitive community in the valley on the planet of Isis where the President will not tolerate anyone who questions the strict laws and taboos he invented. But will Jody survive the journey to Upper Isis, and meet the Guardian himself – the Shining One – and Olwen, and thus learn the truth about Isis and her own people?

'A superb sequel (**to The Keeper of the Isis Light**) showing what Science Fiction can be all about.'

The Guardia

Space Trap

There was blackness with no space and time, no breath and heartbeat . . . her throat had shrunk into a hard knot the way it does during a nightmare.

But it wasn't a dream. When she comes to her senses, Valerie is a prisoner, crouched on the floor of a cage and surrounded by people poking at her through the bars – strange people with snails' eyes, waving about on stalks.

And she knows she has been a victim of the Space Trap. Spirited millions of parsecs away from her home galaxy to an outlaw planet, Valerie must escape or spend the rest of her life in the primate zoo – or worse, become the subject of terrible experiments in the humanoid laboratory.

But first, she must discover the secret of the Space Trap . . .

The Isis Pedlar

Michael Joseph Flynn's devious plans to cheat and corrupt the inhabitants of the planet Isis are on the verge of success. Flynn's magic firestone, his strangely delicious Ambrosia, the Forever Machine: all are irresistible to the simple agricultural community, which easily falls prey to the sorcery of its smooth-talking foreign visitor. Only Mike's daughter, Moira, can show up her shameful father in his true light. David N'Kumo, great-grandson of one of the original settlers, becomes her ally – but even with his help, will Moira be able to avert disaster?

'Monica Hughes . . . light years ahead.'
  Times Educational Supplement

DEVIL ON MY BACK

The computer is your memory and mine. With every pak you access you become closer to the ideal of a perfect thinking being.

In Arc One, knowledge is power, and the Young Lords are trained to possess it. But accessing is dangerous. Failures are marched away from their terminals for reprocessing. Their brains will be wrecked for ever: they will become slaves.

Son of Overlord, Tomi dreads Access Day as much as he longs to graduate and become a New Lord. But fate has something else to teach Tomi: the shattering truth behind the tyrannical computer control system of Arc One.

SANDWRITER

prequel to The Promise

Antia, Princess of Komilant and Kamalant, finds the island desert of Roshan a hostile and alien place. The heat, the barren landscape and unfriendly inhabitants all make her feel very alone. But Antia has an important mission. Her beloved tutor, Eskoril, has asked her to discover the secret at the heart of Roshan – and she is determined to succeed.

Soon she finds herself at the very centre of dramatic events. For Roshan is the setting for a bitter and deadly struggle for power . . .

THE PROMISE

'A young man of about fifteen or sixteen stepped forward. He was tall, sunburnt, his hair bleached gold by the sun. As he stood at the foot of her throne, Rania could see that his hands, holding a small box, trembled slightly.

"Here . . ." His voice was rough, just breaking. "Here, Highness, this is for you."'

Atbin's birthday present to Princess Rania is a reminder to her parents of a promise, made long ago, which they must now fulfil. For Sandwriter, the mysterious woman who holds the safety of Rokam in her hand, has chosen the young princess to be her successor.

Rania must live with Sandwriter in the harsh desert of Roshan, learning the secrets of Rokam through years of contemplation and hardship. But when chance throws Rania and Atbin together again, she is faced with an agonising choice . . .

Sequel to *Sandwriter*.

A Selected List of Fiction from Mammoth

While every effort is made to keep prices low, it is sometimes necessary to increase prices at short notice. Mammoth Books reserves the right to show new retail prices on covers which may differ from those previously advertised in the text or elsewhere.

The prices shown below were correct at the time of going to press.

☐	416 13972 8	**Why the Whales Came**	Michael Morpurgo £2.50
☐	7497 0034 3	**My Friend Walter**	Michael Morpurgo £2.50
☐	7497 0035 1	**The Animals of Farthing Wood**	Colin Dann £2.99
☐	7497 0136 6	**I Am David**	Anne Holm £2.50
☐	7497 0139 0	**Snow Spider**	Jenny Nimmo £2.50
☐	7497 0140 4	**Emlyn's Moon**	Jenny Nimmo £2.25
☐	7497 0344 X	**The Haunting**	Margaret Mahy £2.25
☐	416 96850 3	**Catalogue of the Universe**	Margaret Mahy £1.95
☐	7497 0051 3	**My Friend Flicka**	Mary O'Hara £2.99
☐	7497 0079 3	**Thunderhead**	Mary O'Hara £2.99
☐	7497 0219 2	**Green Grass of Wyoming**	Mary O'Hara £2.99
☐	416 13722 9	**Rival Games**	Michael Hardcastle £1.99
☐	416 13212 X	**Mascot**	Michael Hardcastle £1.99
☐	7497 0126 9	**Half a Team**	Michael Hardcastle £1.99
☐	416 08812 0	**The Whipping Boy**	Sid Fleischman £1.99
☐	7497 0035 5	**The Lives of Christopher Chant**	Diana Wynne-Jones £2.50
☐	7497 0164 1	**A Visit to Folly Castle**	Nina Beachcroft £2.25

All these books are available at your bookshop or newsagent, or can be ordered direct from the publisher. Just tick the titles you want and fill in the form below.

Mandarin Paperbacks, Cash Sales Department, PO Box 11, Falmouth, Cornwall TR10 9EN.

Please send cheque or postal order, no currency, for purchase price quoted and allow the following for postage and packing:

UK   80p for the first book, 20p for each additional book ordered to a maximum charge of £2.00.

BFPO   80p for the first book, 20p for each additional book.

Overseas   £1.50 for the first book, £1.00 for the second and 30p for each additional book including Eire   thereafter.

NAME (Block letters) ....

ADDRESS ....

....

....